THE TEMPLE OF YESTERDAY—

The room was small and shaped like a pentagon. A shelf was in each corner and on four of the shelves were skulls that seemed made of glass. Cautiously, Tony picked one up. He saw that it was not glass but crystal.

"I have seen an identical one in Mexico City," Manny said breathlessly.

"What does it mean?" Christine asked him.

"I don't know. The arguments about the crystal skulls have gone on for many years."

"I do not like this room," their guide said with a shiver. "What can a skull mean but death?"

"I have never seen a room like this before," Manny said. "When we return to London, I shall get funding and come back and resolve all the mysteries."

"Is that what you're planning?" Christine asked. "It seems exciting."

"Of course it is exciting. And you shall come back here with me." Manny clapped his hands together, clasping one in the other. And that was when the world changed. . . .

AGE OF
DINOSAURS #1
TYRANNOSAURUS REX

BY

J.F. RIVKIN

A ROC BOOK

ROC
Published by the Penguin Group
Penguin Books USA Inc., 375 Hudson Street,
New York, New York 10014, U.S.A.
Penguin Books Ltd, 27 Wrights Lane,
London W8 5TZ, England
Penguin Books Australia Ltd, Ringwood,
Victoria, Australia
Penguin Books Canada Ltd, 10 Alcorn Avenue,
Toronto, Ontario, Canada M4V 3B2
Penguin Books (N.Z.) Ltd, 182–190 Wairau Road,
Auckland 10, New Zealand

Penguin Books Ltd, Registered Offices:
Harmondsworth, Middlesex, England

First published by Roc, an imprint of New American Library,
a division of Penguin Books USA Inc.

First Printing, October, 1992
10 9 8 7 6 5 4 3 2 1

 REGISTERED TRADEMARK—MARCA REGISTRADA

Printed in the United States of America

TYRANNOSAURUS REX

PROLOGUE

Kuluene district, Matto Grosso State,
August 18, 1925
    Cheeky,
    Success! What I have to tell you is so won-
drous that I, who have seen it, doubt my own
senses. In this uncharted land, near the banks
of the Kuluene River, we have found an ancient
city. The treasures it contains will change the
very foundations of the way we understand the
world.
    Lest you think me delirious with fever, let me
tell you, briefly, what has happened. Whilst
travelling down the Kuliseu River, we encountered the Yanomani, a fierce tribe of Indians
who inhabit these parts. They told us stories of
a great and holy place, where spirits dwelt.
They refused to take us until Jack managed to
cure one of the chief's sons of fever with our
stock of quinine (we haven't a tablet left).
    The chief, Izarari, then agreed to act as guide.
After a long journey by boat, we arrived. The
people who built this city were plainly of Mayan heritage. Everywhere are great stelae,
tombs, and temples, all ornately carved with
the symbols we have seen on so many Mayan

constructions. This is the first time we have seen evidence that the Mayans came so far into South America.

At the center of the city is a massive temple, pyramidal in shape, and within, a single pentagonal room, ten meters across. On four of the five corners is a shelf, and on each shelf rests a human skull made, not of bone, but of some sort of crystal.

And now, I come to the portion of the story which transcends the boundaries of our mundane world and reaches into that unknown territory we call the supernatural.

In the temple our servant, Cuyaba, who has remained with us throughout this long journey, clapped his hands together to kill one of the hordes of stinging flies that infest this country. Before the sound had died away, he vanished completely—utterly—as though he had never been! I need hardly explain our astonishment.

We looked in vain for some sort of trapdoor, crawling on our knees to sound the stone floor, but we could find nothing. Then, as suddenly as he had disappeared, he was back, raving of terrible monsters tall as trees and demons that flew shrieking in the skies.

I will write no more of what we discovered. Suffice it to say that we have plumbed the secrets of this place. When we return, it will be with such a tale to tell as will astonish and amaze the world for many a long year to come.

Jack and I are well enough, although somewhat tired and thin from the rigors of the journey. I am quite worried about Raleigh, whose foot is badly infected. Blood poisoning is on all our minds, although we do not speak of it.

I will entrust this letter to Cuyaba. He has no desire to remain here and has agreed to deliver this letter to the missionaries living at the head-waters of the Xingu.

Your affectionate husband,
Percy

Lips swollen, delirious with fever, Cuyaba lay still in the boat. His breathing was shallow, labored. The boat was snagged in the weeds, but he had no strength to free it. Through dull eyes he watched as the sun's light, always pale and slightly green because of the thick jungle, faded into nothingness.

Was it night or death that blinded him? The distinction was unimportant. He knew that for him the two were one and the same. His mind turned away from worldly matters to matters of the spirit. The white men's paper, their urgent words, was forgotten. He wondered if the land he had glimpsed in the temple was the land of the dead. He steeled his soul for the great journey that lay before him. With a last hoarse gasp, he died.

1

The gigantic beast curved its serpentine neck around the tree and snapped at the man caught halfway up the trunk. "My God, don't leave me," he shrieked, but his companions ran on, desperate to escape from the nightmare that hunted them.

The beast lunged again and snatched the man up with its pointed teeth. The mouth clamped down. He gave a horrible scream that ascended in pitch like a siren gone mad. Then there was an abrupt, dreadful silence. The rest of the crew plunged ahead blindly, going deeper into the jungle.

"Honestly, Chris, how can you watch that juvenile drivel?" Tony complained. He looked at the pizza sitting in its greasy box and wrinkled his nose. "What's on this?"

"Feta cheese, garlic, anchovies, and onions." She took a slice and shoveled half of it into her mouth. "Have a piece—it's my favorite."

He grimaced. "No, I think not. I don't understand why you always order *your* favorite. Why don't you ever order mine? You know I try to stay away from these exotic combinations. You've absolutely no sense of tradition."

She turned to him and said, "You're a hypocrite, Tony."

"I beg your pardon?"

"Don't think I don't know about you getting up in the morning before I do and eating all the anchovies off the leftovers."

He opened his mouth to protest but she cut him off. "There's no point in denying it—I've suspected it for ages. Last week I proved it because I counted them before I went to bed and then again when I got up. You'd eaten six anchovies. So let's just drop this holier-than-thou nonsense." She gave him a smug little smile and turned back to the television.

He looked shocked. "I'd never have thought you could be so petty, Chris. It's a terrible revelation to me to realize that what's on your mind before we go to bed is the safekeeping of your anchovies. It puts our relationship in a whole new light. I think it's very cold-blooded of you."

He shrugged, took a piece of pizza, and gave his attention to the movie, watching as King Kong shook the remnants of the ship's crew off a huge log and into the canyon that gaped below.

"Why are Americans so obsessed with size?" he demanded. "Everything has to be large with them. Even their fantasies are colossal—giant apes clutching voluptuous blondes and climbing huge, phallic structures. Why can't they be satisfied with vampires and mad slashers, the way we are?

"I'm sure Freud would have written about it. He would have told us that American men have

never really dealt with the rivalry that exists between their fathers and themselves. So, as a
consequence, they are insecure about their own
virility and the size of their genitals.''

"Shut up, Tony," Christine said gently.

"Furthermore," he continued, unperturbed,
"what would he tell us about women who are
entranced by visions of being carried off by
large, hairy beasts?"

"He would tell us that they're being driven
mad with frustration by lovers who indulge in
orgies of pop psychology. You know, the cin-
ema down the road is still open. If you rush
you can catch the last showing—it should just
suit your frame of mind. It's some foreign thing
absolutely fraught with psychic tensions.''

"That's all right, darling.'' He put an arm
around her shoulder and watched the great ape
bellow and beat his chest. "I'm satisfied with
what's on the bill here later this evening.'' He
nuzzled her ear. "I'll be Tarzan and you can be
Jane.'' He paused. "Or would you prefer that
I be Cheetah?''

She smiled and took another bite of pizza.
"Wait till you see the part where King Kong
fights off the *Tyrannosaurus*. It's one of my favorite bits. Do you think I look like Fay Wray?''

Christine Fawcett was twenty-nine-years old
and, as her mother, Lily, was fond of remind-
ing her, "thirty was looming on the horizon.''
She always spoke this phrase in a tone that
Christine felt was more properly suited to na-
tional disasters such as nuclear war or losing
the World Cup.

She was of average height, with short brown hair and big brown eyes. Her mother was always begging her to wear contacts instead of her glasses, saying that Christine's eyes were one of her best features. Christine felt that people said this when there was nothing else in particular to compliment. Her mother never said what her other best features were.

After much careful scrutiny of her own reflection, Christine had decided that she was pretty enough, but no showstopper. Most people thought she was "sweet-looking"—which always left her with thoughts of plastic surgery.

The conversation Christine had with her mother that morning over breakfast in a fashionable restaurant had been a representative one.

"My dear," her mother said, "it's all very well to have a career, but there are other things that matter just as much."

"I wouldn't know," Christine answered, "since I don't have a career. I don't know anything about cartography and I don't know anything about business practices. All I do sitting on the board of the company is exactly that—sit. I'm sure the board members have mentioned that to you more than once."

"They're worried about you, darling. They were all friends of your father and they're concerned for you. They just want you to find yourself. Alistair dandled you on his knee when you were a toddler."

"I'm sure he'd be perfectly willing to resume the practice if he thought I'd let him. I know he's dandled a secretary or two. And please stop talking about 'finding myself', Mother. It makes me feel like a piece of luggage that's been mislaid. I know exactly what I am—I'm a parasite, living off the hard-won gains of others. I enjoy it very much. There's no need to worry. Most people would be wildly envious."

"You can't throw your life away like that, darling. Everyone needs useful work."

"Why?"

"Stop being contradictory, Christine. Ever since you were a child you'd always bring up these irrelevant questions and go to ridiculous lengths just to prove a point. I remember when you were six and put the frog into your milk. You insisted it was there and when we said it was impossible, you argued and demanded to know why it was impossible."

"I argued because I was right. There was a frog in my milk and so it clearly was possible."

"Yes, but that's not the point. The point is that putting a frog into—" Her mother stopped herself abruptly. "There, you see," she said, "you're doing it again. You're making me lose track of what I was talking about. No, I insist on knowing how you've been spending your time."

"I simply brightened the corners where I sat and gladdened the hearts of those who met me."

Lily snorted. "Don't be absurd, Christine. The last time you brightened anything was when you were seven and smeared red gelatin all over the nursery walls—that is the extent of your ability to brighten. Really, you were a difficult child. Now tell me what you've done this week."

Christine rolled her eyes. "I don't know. Let me see . . ." She began ticking off events on her fingers. "I slept through one of the board meetings but managed to stay awake for another. Several members thanked me afterwards. It's nice to know one's efforts are appreciated. I also completed some very intricate doodles." She paused and stared thoughtfully at her sausages.

"Oh yes," she resumed, giving her mother a dazzling smile, "I did manage to learn that something we're doing has gone up and that something else has gone down. Also, we're thinking about a joint project with an entity called Amalgamated Porcupine—at least I think that was the name. Then, I read some new books and reread some old ones, and . . ."

"Have you seen any more of that nice young man . . . what was his name?"

"Ah, now we get to the meat of the matter. Which one? There's so many of them."

"There are not. There are hardly ever any. You're almost a recluse. Not to mention that the last man you went out with was a socialist. The military fellow is the one I mean, the lean one with the craggy face. I always find lean men with craggy faces to be very attractive—they look so competent."

"You mean Lieutenant Mark Anthony Blondell, late of the Special Air Services," Christine answered, saluting her mother smartly. "He's not military anymore—he's unemployed. He's a member of the great unwashed."

"Yes, that's him. I'm sure he'll settle into something very distinguished. Perhaps he'll get a government post. Are you still seeing him?"

"Oh, yes. He's coming over this evening, in fact."

Her mother beamed. "That's very nice. And what are you two planning on doing—off to a show, I suppose?"

"No, just a quiet evening, I think."

"Will you make dinner? I have some wonderful recipes I could lend you."

"This is going to be a catered affair, Mother. Nick's down the road will provide the comestibles. They've the best pizza for blocks around."

Her mother stared at her, her face frozen in an expression of despair. "I wish I thought you were joking," she said after a long pause. "Of course, you're not."

Christine took a forkful of eggs. "Do you think feta cheese and mozzarella is too much of a good thing?" she asked brightly.

Christine lay quietly in Tony's arms, listening to the sounds of London traffic that rattled the bedroom window. "Tony?" she whispered.

"Mmmm?"

"Are you asleep?"

"Yes."

"Good. Mother thinks you have a craggy face and look competent."

"She's right on both counts. Your mother is a very observant woman. My incredible competence is only matched by my extraordinary cragginess. They've scheduled an expedition to climb the left side of my nose next June, weather permitting.''

"You're an idiot. Do you want to know what I did today?''

"No, I want to go to sleep. Tell me what you did today tomorrow.''

"I went through some of my father's papers and I started reading Grandfather's diaries.''

"Ah, Percy Fawcett, the great explorer.'' He rolled over on his side.

"You know, Father always thought Percy or Uncle Jack might still be alive.''

"Christine, that's absurd. Your father was eaten up by guilt because he didn't go wandering off with them to die in that godforsaken Brazilian jungle. Believing they were still alive made him feel better. It's that simple. Good night.''

"I don't understand your attitude, Tony. You talk like a sociologist, not a man of action. What did the SAS *do* in the Falklands—psychoanalyze the Argentinians into submission?''

Tony rolled over again to look at her. "Hardly, my dear, but there's a chance we could have, if we'd only known what we were doing. Their morale was as fragile as blown glass. Don't underestimate the power of the mind. Most countries today invest quite a bit of money in psychological operations.''

"Well, it's hardly the stuff they make movies about. I can just see the lot of you over there asking some poor South American about his mother. No wonder they shot at you.''

"You must realize the SAS doesn't want their

officers to be chest-beating Rambos rushing off
with their Sten guns. Mental toughness is the
ideal as much as physical stamina. Certainly,
we were supposed to be able to recognize im-
mature, romantic nonsense when we heard it.
That's the way to get your men senselessly
killed. It's cool thinking that keeps you alive,
not bravado or emotional impulses."

"Thank you for that lecture on military matters, but it's beside the point. We were talking
about my father. I hope you're not saying he
was nothing but an overgrown adolescent.
That's not fair, Tony, and it's not true."

He pulled her toward him. "I'm sorry, darling. But Brian wasn't a man particularly at ease
with himself—you know that better than I. His
whole life was colored by a sense of dissatisfac-
tion. He simply couldn't admit that his father
and brother had died over there and that there
was nothing he could do about it."

Christine sighed. "You're right, of course. I
think it was his lameness. He never really got
over it. Percy and Jack would go off exploring
and he couldn't keep up with them. They got
all the glory. And then he started the company
and was stuck in his office.

"It was hard for him. He had their love for
adventure and travel but couldn't really hack
the life—his health wouldn't stand it. It's no
surprise he ended up making maps for a living.
He used to stare at them and trace out Percy's
routes."

"He did well for himself financially," Tony
replied, "and for the entire family. That's no
small achievement. The world's become a place

for those who sit in offices, not for those who want to dash off exploring the great unknown. Percy was one of the last of a dying breed—the intrepid British explorer. He could never have made it in Brian's world.

"For one thing, there's bloody little of the great unknown left. You know better than I what satellites have told us about the planet and how much of it's been mapped out by Landsat. And for another thing, the solitary explorer is a thing of the past. Everything's all publicity and grants and newspaper articles and air-dropped supplies. And don't forget the political aspects of it all. You have to consider everything—the destruction of native cultures, the environmental impact, government politics. The global village is a complicated piece of real estate. Brian wasn't the only one who felt the walls closing in."

Christine looked over at him, trying to see his face in the dark bedroom. His voice sounded clipped and harsh and she felt the tension in his lean, compact body. "Do you wish you'd stayed in the service, Tony? Ordinary life must seem frightfully dull after the commandos."

"No, I don't. I'm thirty-two-years old. It's time I took on the world on my own terms. I'll make a place for myself in it. I've no more patience with military politics and global insanity."

Christine was silent for a moment. A vague idea was forming in the back of her mind. "I think I'll do a bit more digging around in the family papers," she said. "There are things stored away in the attic I've never seen. Per-

haps there's some clue as to what happened to
Percy and Jack. Maybe I could write a book.''

Tony yawned. ''Perhaps, but don't be disappointed if all you find is old laundry lists and
letters from Great-aunt Matilda about the rising
price of soap.''

''I don't have a Great-aunt Matilda.''

''Everyone has a Great-aunt Matilda. She
wears sensible shoes, dead animals around her
neck, clips all the coupons, and disapproves of
everything.''

''Oh, you mean Aunt Lucy.''

''Precisely.'' He rolled back onto his other
side. ''Let me know if you find the guidebook
to Atlantis or Mu or the City That Time Forgot
in the Lost Valley of the Time Machine.''

''I'll do better than that—I'll book you a room
with a view.''

''Just check that they take charge cards—I
don't like carrying too much cash.''

She kissed him gently on the ear. ''Good
night, Tony.''

The next morning, Christine began rummaging through the trunks that held the family papers. Although the British Museum had wanted
them, Brian had been adamant about not giving them up. He'd even made it a stipulation
of his will. He felt there were secrets in them
that should be kept from the public's prying
eyes.

Pawing through the dusty packets of letters
and yellowing journals, trying not to sneeze in
case she blew the dust about even more, Christine briefly wondered about Brian's sanity. She

couldn't imagine any secrets in this moldering pile of paper.

At the bottom of the trunk, she found a large, oddly shaped parcel wrapped in brown paper. With a grunt, she heaved it out of the chest.

Scribbled on the wrapping was a message in her father's precise handwriting. It said, "Received January 28, 1926, sent from Rio de Janeiro by missionaries who received it from an Indian. No further information available; have been unable to locate missionaries."

"God," she thought, as she gingerly unwrapped it, "I hope it's not shrunken heads."

Once she'd opened it, she saw that it was a bone of some sort—a very large bone. She turned it around and about, examining it. It looked like nothing she'd ever seen.

"Of course, my knowledge of bones is rather limited to chicken legs and the like," she thought. "I wonder what it is. It's bigger than anything I've ever seen in the butcher's. And why in heaven's name would someone want to drag it all over South America, or bother sending it back to England?"

She skimmed through the packets of letters, trying to find an explanation, but there was nothing.

Tony Blondell, late of the Special Air Services, sat at his desk, staring at his computer screen. His flat was a small one, but looked very tidy. Books were lined neatly on their shelves and the pictures hung straight on the walls. The only note of disorder was the wastebasket which held a mound of crumpled paper.

Laboriously, Tony typed, "Career Objectives: To secure a position that would best use my organizational and managerial skills—"

"Damn it to living hell," he said, bringing his hand down on the keyboard. The computer beeped hysterically.

Tony ran his fingers through his hair. "Who am I trying to fool? I don't want to be some sort of pencil-pushing manager. I'd lose my mind." He looked at his reflection in the screen. "I'm thirty-two and I still don't know what I want to be when I grow up."

He picked up a pencil and chewed on the tip for a bit. Then he picked up a pad and began to write.

Knowledge: Extensive combat experience; survival training; squadron leader.

Possible position: SAS commander; mercenary; assassin; Robin Hood; right-wing political candidate.

Objections: I've done the first and I'm heartily sick of it. The others don't appeal to me and my legs are too thin to look good in green tights anyways.

He tapped the pencil against his chin for a moment and began to write again. He began a new category.

Personality: Intelligent, sense of humor—

He threw down the pencil. "This is beginning to sound like an ad in the personals column. Single male, intelligent, sense of humor seeks single female. Enjoys the outdoors and sex."

He began writing again, adding to his list that he possessed qualities of callousness, cold objectivity, and a hatred of bureaucracy. Satisfied that he had at least made himself into a much less pleasant person, he got up to get a drink.

The telephone rang. "Blondell Assassination Bureau," he answered. "No murder too small. Anthony Blondell speaking."

"What kind of way is that to answer the phone?" Christine demanded.

"I've decided to go into business for myself. After thoroughly reviewing my credentials, I've resolved to go into competition with Murder Incorporated. I'll do the work for half the price in half the time. Also, I'm running a two-for-one special at the moment. Are you interested? No minor functionary too minor, no major too major."

"I take it the resume writing isn't going well?"

"Can you picture me as Robin Hood?"

"No. I can only picture Erroll Flynn. He had infinitely better legs."

Tony sighed. "Unfortunately, I came to the same conclusion." He snapped his fingers. "I've got it, Chris. Why don't we emigrate?"

"What? To where?"

"Australia, of course. Just think of it—the great outback, braving the elements, just a man, his sheep, and his woman."

"I can't say I think much of your priorities," Christine said. "I don't fancy taking second place to a piece of mutton. Besides, I don't want to go to Australia. I object on moral grounds to places with hot, sunny climates. I think they give you a warped outlook on life."

"Christine, you are of absolutely no help.

You don't like my ideas and you don't like my legs. Why the hell are you calling me?''

''I wanted to tell you that I've been looking through the family memorabilia and I've found something rather odd. In fact, I've unearthed a bone.''

''What sort of bone? You mean a piece of a skeleton?''

''That's what a bone is, isn't it? In my experience it is, at any rate. The head bone's connected to the neck bone, the neck bone's connected to the . . .''

''Yes, yes, thank you, Chris. I mean, what sort of bone is it?''

''A very, very large one.''

''Good God, it sounds like you've found Aunt Matilda herself, instead of just her letters. Maybe Brian got sick of her constant moralizing and did away with her. You may have found more than a bone, my dear. It may be the proverbial skeleton in the closet.''

''I doubt it very much. This is some sort of animal. I can't imagine what kind. Do you think Percy might have come across a dead elephant in his travels?''

''Percy could have come across anything and probably did. Wasn't there any sort of letter with it?''

''My father wrote a note on the wrapping saying some Brazilian missionaries had sent it to him in '26. That was the year Percy disappeared.''

''Hmmm . . . I suppose it's all very sinister. What do you want me to do about it?''

"I thought I'd take it to the Natural History Museum tomorrow and have Stephen take a look at it. Would you want to come along?"

"Who is Stephen?"

"Stephen Lesley, the naturalist. He was a friend of father's."

"Can't say I've ever heard of him. Aren't naturalists the ones who run around without any clothes?"

"Very funny. I think the term is either naturist or nudist, as you well know."

"I suppose I'd better go with you. It sounds a suspicious profession. Suppose you were abducted by the Creature from the Black Lagoon? I'd never forgive myself."

"I'm going to the museum, not the aquarium. What you're really saying is going with me is better than working on your resume."

"You're a cruel woman, darling. Whoever told you that honesty was a virtue?"

"I'll be around about nine tomorrow, if that's all right?"

"Why don't you spend the night? That way you'd already be here."

"Sorry. I'm going to continue digging and you have to brood about your future. Mother thinks you should get some sort of government post. She'll be very disappointed if you turn out to be a layabout."

"Well," he sighed, "I certainly wouldn't want to disappoint someone's mother. What do *you* think I'm good at, Chris?"

Christine laughed. "I'll tell you tomorrow. I'm not sure I'm allowed to talk about those things over the phone. Good-bye, darling. See you tomorrow.''

''Wait,'' he said, ''I'm not done procrastin . . .'' But she had already hung up. Sighing, he turned back to the computer.

2

As Christine drove to the museum, Tony looked at the bone, eyeing it from every angle. "Certainly is large," he pronounced.

"Thank you very much. I'd managed to discover that on my own. I was hoping you'd know what it was."

"Haven't the faintest," Tony answered cheerfully. "But I certainly hope I never get on the wrong side of the bastard who's walking around without it." He rewrapped the bone and rested it on his knee.

Christine sniffed. "I doubt if the owner can be counted among the living. It must be something from a rhino or an elephant. I'm sure Stephen can tell us."

"He won't tell us a thing if we don't get there alive," Tony said, as he watched the landscape go by in a single, dismaying blur. "Speed limits aren't optional, you know. You're supposed to obey them whether you feel like it or not."

"Everyone drives like this in France," Christine said.

"What does that have to do with . . ."

"There's the turnoff right ahead," she broke in.

The Natural History Museum, a masterpiece of Victorian architecture made of blue-and-cream brick, with its pinnacles and towers, looked like a cathedral. Christine swerved wildly to the left and into the parking lot, coolly ignoring a passing motorist's description of her ancestry. She hopped out of the car, singing softly under her breath, "Dem bones, dem bones, dem dry bones . . ."

"What sort of naturalist is this Lesley fellow?" Tony asked, as they walked inside.

"An ornithologist, I think. He's potty about birds."

Tony laughed. "Talk about Big Bird. You don't think this is from some sort of oversized chicken, do you?"

"Of course not, but it's a start at least. He's the only person I know who's at all knowledgeable in dead animals—except the butcher, of course." She paused for a moment and stared at Tony. "I wonder if I should have brought it to him first. I'm going to feel like a total fool if this thing turns out to be a piece of a cow."

"That would be funny. Does this Lesley fellow have a sense of humor?"

Christine pursed her lips. "Not so's I've noticed."

They found Stephen Lesley in a gallery filled with birds frozen in attitudes of arrested flight or peaceful repose, their feathers glittering in the dim museum light like unmined gems. Some were poised over clutches of eggs that were smeared or lined, blotched or spotted with greens, whites, purples, and browns.

Stephen Lesley was a man in his sixties with a round face and eyes that peered out from behind round spectacles. He was short, paunchy, and dressed in a suit of dusty brown. Influenced by his surroundings, the word that first came to Tony's mind was "owlish."

"Kites," Stephen said to them, without looking up. "Have you ever seen their like?" He gestured vaguely to one of the displays. "And over here, blue and yellow macaws, then terns, a ringed kingfisher, nightjars. The birds of the Amazon. Magnificent, don't you think?"

"They're gorgeous," Christine answered. "Is this your latest exhibit?"

He nodded, then looked up to examine her more closely. "But since when are you interested in birds? I thought you weren't interested in anything."

"This is Mark Anthony Blondell, Stephen," Christine said, ignoring the question and the statement together.

"Gave up on that socialist fellow, did you?" He examined Tony. "You, are you a bird man?" he demanded.

"Well, not as such," Tony said, floundering for an answer. "I've been known to feed the odd pigeon or two."

Stephen gave him a look which told Tony he had been examined, classified, and relegated to some sort of subspecies which had no importance to the planet. He decided to say as little as possible.

"I've come to see you about something I found in Grandfather's things," Christine said.

Stephen snorted. "Percy didn't care about birds. Went to some of the most fabulous places for birds in the world and never took any notes of any importance. I can't understand the man. Now, von Humboldt, he was a man for birds— of course he was before Percy's time, but still, you would have thought Percy would have taken it as a challenge. He never discovered a single species." He was silent for a moment. "Well?"

"Sorry?" Christine asked.

"Well, what did you find? And why bring it to me if it's not a bird?"

"It's this," Christine said, motioning for Tony to lay the bone on a case. Gingerly, he did so, pulling back the wrappings.

"My God, it's gigantic," Stephen said, gently running a finger along its contours. He leaned over it, examining the bone more closely. "I haven't a clue what it is, but I suppose you thought I could put you in touch with someone who would?"

"I was rather hoping that," Christine said.

"Come along then," Stephen said, and starting shuffling off down the hall. Christine snatched up the bone and she and Tony followed him down the hall.

They ended up in the basement, in a dingy lab lit by florescent bulbs. Plaster dust covered everything. The room seemed a combination of a quarry and a graveyard. Chunks of rock were lined up on a counter, intermixed with skulls and several long bones.

Hunched over a table, a woman was busily scraping at a rock with a dental pick. Her movements were precise and meticulous and her expression absorbed and peaceful. Beside her were some small brushes, more picks, and tweezers. She looked up when they came in, and smiled. "What is it, Stevie?"

"Dr. Dorothy Langley," Stephan said, indulging in another vague gesture. "She runs our paleontology department. These people have a rather large bone with them, Dottie. Perhaps you'd care to take a look? They certainly don't know anything about it and neither do I. But I can tell you one thing—whatever it belonged to never flew." He seemed to think this enormously funny.

Tony handed the bone to her and her eyes widened. "Oh my, but where did you get this? It's a dorsal vertebra of a *Tyrannosaurus rex*."

"A what?" Christine gasped. "Not that creature that's in *King Kong*? Surely you're mistaken?"

Dr. Langley shrugged. "I think not. I've dug up several myself in Mongolia, you know."

"Percy was never in Mongolia," Christine objected. "This came from Brazil."

"There have been a few fossils found there of related species," Dr. Langley said, "but no one's ever found any sign of old *T. rex* himself. Perhaps he bought it from a collector. How did you get it?"

Christine told her the story and showed her the note on the wrapping paper. The doctor was intrigued. "Will you leave it with me for a few days?" she asked. "I'd like to run a few tests and show it to some of my colleagues."

Christine agreed, and Dr. Langley said, "Why don't you come see the model of the whole thing? We've one on exhibit. They're quite impressive."

She took them into a long gallery filled with dinosaur skeletons. Looming over them all was the *Tyrannosaurus rex*. "This is a replica of a complete skeleton found at Hell's Creek, Montana in the States," Dr. Langley said. "The original's in the American Museum of Natural History in New York City."

"That sounds like an appropriate place for a beast like this," Tony said, staring up at it.

"Where?" Christine asked. "Hell Creek or New York?" She was amused to note that he had the same expression on his face as several toddlers who were grouped around the model's base.

"Either," he answered. "I'll bet that thing never worried about getting mugged after dark. When did it live?"

"In the late Cretaceous, about sixty million years ago—the last age of the dinosaurs. It was quite a formidable hunter," Dr. Langley said. "The name means tyrant lizard, and you can see why. It stands about eighteen feet high, thirty-nine feet long, and weighs approximately fifteen thousand pounds.

"Our theories about dinosaurs are undergoing all sorts of challenges, you know, and we're changing our thinking about most of them." Her voice had taken on a warm, excited tone, and her face looked quite animated. Christine, who had grown up in a house frequented by academics, knew all the signs. She braced herself for a lecture.

"For instance," Doctor Langley continued, "instead of being a lumbering, clumsy brute, many people think *Tyrannosaurus* could have gone upwards of forty miles an hour, despite its size and weight."

She stooped under the guardrail and went up to the model. Standing beside it made her look like a dwarf. She ran her finger along the edge of the animal's lower leg. "This bony ridge here is positively massive compared to that of even an elephant's. That means quite powerful knees and calves and *that* means a fast runner."

Pointing up to the skull, she continued, "The teeth are gigantic and thick, capable of resisting exceptional forces when biting. Also, the skull isn't made up of separate pieces, linked together but instead is a unified whole. It's very solidly constructed with no moving parts except at the joint of the jaw. The compartments in the skull and in the lower jaw that housed the muscles are enlarged more than in any other predator.

"It also has a well-developed hinge between the front and back sections of its lower jaws. When *Tyrannosaurus* bolted down huge pieces of meat, the bottom jaw flexed from side to side to widen the gullet.

"Another interesting point is that early predatory dinosaurs possessed very little depth perception because their eyes faced directly sideways. The tyrannosaur's snout, if you'll notice, is pinched in to clear its field of vision. And its eyes face forward to give some overlap between visual fields from the left and right eyes. That would permit stereoscopic vision and that means the ability to judge space and distance well.'' _

"Past tense, Dottie, past tense," Stephen broke in. She looked at him quizzically. "You're talking about something that's been long dead as if it's going to show up under the Albert Memorial." He turned to Christine. "They turned into birds, you know."

"Excuse me?" Christine asked. She looked at the massive skeleton. "It doesn't look very flight worthy."

"Oh, there's quite a bit of evidence to show that birds evolved from dinosaurs," Stephen answered. "They have similar ankle joints, hind feet, compact bipedal body. . . . Huxley wrote about it extensively."

Christine looked at the model again and got a sudden image of *Tyrannosaurus rex* with a toothy grin, wings, and a halo, hovering in the air and strumming a harp. She giggled and realized that Stephen was staring at her disapprovingly.

"Sorry, Stephen, it's just difficult to picture."

He snorted. "Are you done, Dottie? I'm sure these young people would like to go off to a rock-and-roll concert or something educational of that nature."

"Stop being so cantankerous, Stephen. Don't pay him any mind, he works at being an eccentric professor," she said to Christine and Tony. "In any case, I didn't mean to ramble on. Give me your number so that I can call you in a couple of days and tell you what else I've found out."

"I'm sure it will be exciting," Christine said. "And thank you so much. Good-bye Stephen." She took Tony by the arm. "Come along, love. If we hurry we can catch the Screaming Nymphos concert. But I want to shoot up first."

"What are you thinking?" she asked Tony as they were driving home.

"I was wondering if Stephen and Dr. Langley were sleeping together."

"I was rather wondering that myself. She's very nice. But what do you think about the bone?"

Tony shrugged. "Who knows. I rather doubt that there are dinosaurs wandering around the jungles of Brazil and Percy bagged one. I suppose he got it from some collector, like the good doctor suggested, and sent it back."

"I suppose you're right," Christine said, sounding rather disappointed.

"Well, what did you want the thing to be? It's more exciting than if it were a denuded flank steak. Which reminds me—I'm about two steps away from malnutrition."

Christine sighed. "I don't know what I want. What do you want, Tony?"

"Now that I mention it, a flank steak doesn't sound bad—with some potatoes done all crispy around the edges, a salad, and a good bottle of wine."

"You know what I mean. I'm getting tired of everyone saying that I have no good purpose in life. Mother's bad enough, but now Stephen's doing it—and we don't even know each other very well. I'll bet Lily's been bending his ear.

"And look at you—sitting at home crumpling up your resume, talking about being Robin Hood. What's the matter with us?"

"We're just trying to settle into something. It isn't like I've done nothing with my life, Christine. I spent ten years in the service, if you remember."

"I know, I know. Perhaps I just mean me. Really, I am a bit of a disgrace. I think I envy you those ten years a little."

Tony looked at her in concern. "Buck up, Chris, this isn't like you. You'll find something if you really want to, and so will I. I'm just feeling a little lost right now—in a 'transitional period', I believe is what the shrinks say."

"Sometimes I feel as if my whole life is a transitional period, Tony. Maybe I'm starting to feel my age."

Tony put his arm around her. "You're intelligent, charming, funny, and sexy. How many people can lay claim to all that?"

"Everyone, if you read the personals," she said gloomily.

"Well, I tried," said Tony, shrugging his shoulders. "You know what I think is the matter with you? Low blood sugar. You need a good meal."

"Maybe you're right. Shall we pick up a pizza?"

"The other thing that's the matter with you is you've no taste buds and no eardrums. No, we will not pick up a pizza. I've already told you what I feel like eating. And we'll go to a proper restaurant where you have to use tableware and sit on chairs. I'm tired of eating with my hands like Ug the caveman."

"I have real trouble imagining you roughing it in the service, Tony. You're so fussy."

"Ten years of roughing it is more than enough. I've opted for civilization and all its comforts."

Two days later Dr. Langley called Christine. "Ms. Fawcett, we've discovered several very odd things about the specimen you brought us. It does seem to be what I said . . . the dorsal vertebra of a *Tyrannosaurus rex*. But there are some puzzling characteristics. For one thing, it's not a fossil. It's the very bone."

"I'm sorry," Christine said, "but I don't quite follow."

"You understand that fossils are really perfect imitations of the actual piece? Various minerals replace the original material leaving you with a complete replica. Only here, we haven't the replica—we've the bone itself.

"This does happen on very rare occasions, but there's another problem: the bone isn't old enough. It should be around sixty million years old."

"How old is it?"

"Oh, I can't tell really, but it's clearly contemporary. The dating techniques we use show virtually no carbon-14 decay at all. I'm sorry, Ms. Fawcett, but everything points to this being some sort of hoax. I haven't a clue how it was accomplished, but I'm afraid your grandfather was badly taken in."

"Are you sure? It's hard for me to think anyone got the best of Grandfather."

Dr. Langley laughed. "It's either a fake or there was a *Tyrannosaurus rex* wandering about the Brazillian jungles in the not-so-distant past. Those are the only two alternatives I can think of. You can believe whichever one suits you. Personally, I think it's a counterfeit. Come by and pick it up whenever you like. Stephen sends his regards."

Christine thanked her and slowly hung up the phone. She felt disappointed and a little depressed. Although the rational part of her had never expected the bone to be anything truly remarkable, there was another part of her—the part that secretly still hoped for a genii to someday come out of a bottle or a nymph to show herself in Kensington Gardens—that had indeed expected a miraculous discovery.

A fossil had at least been interesting; but a fake was nothing but a disappointment. There had been a moment when a doorway that led from the mundane world to the fantastic seemed to have been opened, but that door had been slammed shut again.

Idly, she thought of her grandfather. What must it have been like, she wondered, to penetrate to the secret places of the world? Her own life, and the lives of everyone she knew, moved between boundaries as clearly defined as the sidewalks and streets of the city they lived in.

She tried to imagine a life filled with adventure and uncertainty and her mind filled with images from movies and books—*Alan Quartermain, She,* and *King Solomon's Mines.* These were only fantasies of armchair escapism devoured by people whose lives were regulated and constrained by the rules of ordinary life and who, in all probability, would never want to really undergo the rigors of an explorer's life.

People in her own family had experienced the freedom millions of others read about, but her father had only reluctantly discussed his travels in South America. He said that remembering them unsettled him—that real life was here in England, with his business and his family. He had tried to put those journeys away from him and concentrate only on the here and now; but they had nagged at him, haunting him with memories of fiercely colored flowers, strange birds, and of a hidden world lit palely by sea-green light filtering through the overhanging trees.

Christine sat quietly for a time, watching the sun withdraw from her windows and leave the room in twilight. She picked up the phone and dialed. "Tony? It's Chris. Are you busy? Good, pack your kit. We're going to Brazil."

"Christine, you don't know what you're saying!" Tony said rather heatedly. "You've no idea what life in the Brazilian jungles is like. You're not prepared to undertake a project like this. If I'd known you harbored secret ambitions to live out some sort of Edgar Rice Burroughs fantasy, I doubt if I'd ever have taken up with you."

Christine paced back and forth, shaking her head. "I don't expect this to be easy and I'll do what it takes to get prepared. I want this, Tony."

"For God sakes, why?"

"Because I'm restless, or because I'm bored, or because it's in my blood, or because my life feels like a shapeless mess. I don't really know. But I'm sick of myself and of wandering around like a lost lamb looking for its mother. I want to do something different. It's important to me. I want to retrace Grandfather's steps and try to find out where he went. I want to write a book about it. I want people to read it and I want to know that I've got the same stuff in me that he had."

She was talking loudly, counting off her desires by pounding her fist against her palm. "I want you to come with me, Tony. You're the perfect choice with your background, and besides, I don't want to be away from you for so long. But understand this," she said, turning to face him, "I'm going with you or without you. My mind's made up."

Tony looked at the set lines of her mouth and the hard look in her eyes. He had no doubt she meant what she said. "I may not be the best choice," he told her. "I've never been in a jungle. Most of my skills are for arctic terrain."

"You've a cool head. You know how to organize a team and keep discipline. You know how to survive," she answered him. "I can supply willingness and money, but you'll be the real leader, Tony."

He sighed and tried to think. He couldn't let Christine go off without him. And the idea was enticing. Running an expedition in the Brazilian jungles was the stuff of the books he had read as a child. It was a boyhood fantasy taking on flesh. "Our problems will be waiting for us when we get back," he said to her. "We'll still be faced with what we want to do with ourselves, and with the modern world. It's not going to disappear while we're gone."

Christine smiled at him. "It won't disappear, but surely we can put it on hold for a few months? Where's the harm in that?" She looked excitedly at Tony. He was clearly taking her seriously, and his eyes had a far-off expression.

"We'll need help," he said thoughtfully. "And we'll need people with contacts. I wonder if I can get an old friend of mine to come with us. He's spent plenty of time in South and Central America. He's done everything. And I'll need a copy of Percy's route, at least as much of it as anyone knows. Manny's going to want all the facts."

"Talk to him," Christine said eagerly, digging through a pile of papers. "And while you're doing that," she said, taking a deep breath, "I'll tell Mother."

"I beg your pardon? Did I hear you correctly?"

"Yes, Mother. Tony and I are going to Brazil

to try and find out what happened to Percy and Jack."

"Christine, I forbid it. I absolutely refuse to let you go." Her mother's voice rose enough in pitch so that the other diners turned to look at their table. Noticing this, Lily lowered her voice to a tense whisper. She bent over the table toward her daughter. "Where do you come up with these harebrained schemes? Have you lost your mind? There are bugs in those jungles, Christine!"

"Mother, calm down," Christine said in as soothing a voice as she could muster. "It'll be fine. Tony's coming with me—and you know how competent he is."

"I do not know!"

"You said yourself he looked competent."

"Well, what if I did? That doesn't prove a thing. Lots of people look competent and aren't. What competent person would agree to something like this?"

"Mother, people go to Brazil all the time. It's not what it was in Grandfather's day."

"People go to *Rio* all the time. They check into a nice hotel, sit on the beach wearing obscene swimwear, and flirt. That's civilized. Percy did not do these things. The reason he was the first European in all those places was because he went places no other European in his right mind wanted to go. And now you want to do the same thing. Why don't you go skiing in Chamonix instead? That's dangerous, but at least there's plumbing."

"I don't know how to ski," Christine retorted sullenly, crumbling up bits of bread.

"You don't know how to be an explorer, either. Christine, you don't even go to the zoo and you've killed every plant you've ever owned."

"Aren't you curious to find out what happened to Percy and Jack?" Christine asked her. "They are family, after all."

"No one has any doubt what happened to them. They died of some horrid disease or they were murdered. It was bound to happen. And why would I want to risk my only child to find out about two men who were dead, if not buried, fifty years ago?"

Christine took her mother's hand and squeezed it. "I'll be all right, Mother. It really isn't as dangerous as it used to be. I want to trace Percy's steps on his last journey and write about what I find. Maybe it'll be a bestseller." Lily looked as if she were going to cry.

"And Tony does know what he's doing," Christine continued, trying to make her voice as casual and reassuring as she could. "And he has all sorts of friends who've been to Brazil and traveled through the rain forest. He's talking to one of them right now."

Tony had phoned his friend, Manny, and made an appointment to meet him at his club. He only told him that a friend of his, Chris Fawcett, wanted to fund an expedition. He thought he'd leave the details until they met face-to-face.

Manuel Aburto had once been an officer in the Mexican army. His bravery and intelligence were well-known. Also known were his independence, stubbornness, and libidinous nature.

His military career ended rather abruptly when he'd been discovered in bed with his general's wife. The general, Manny's own wife, and his mistress had pooled their resources and hired one of the city's more accomplished toughs to rearrange Manny's body into a pretzellike configuration.

He had escaped and spent the intervening years avoiding Mexico, dropping out of helicopters onto jungle mountains, abseiling into sinkholes and caves, and doing research on his ancestors, the Mayans. He had also given military advice to various groups in Central and South America whose views were somewhat in conflict with those of the reigning powers.

Several governments found him enough of a nuisance to consider that his death would not be a bad thing. Tony, who had met him during the Falklands War, considered him an invaluable resource, a good soldier, a stalwart companion. He could think of no one better to accompany them on the search for Percy and Jack Fawcett.

Tony found him sitting quietly in a corner of the central quadrangle of the club, sipping a glass of mineral water. Manuel Aburto was a strikingly handsome man, with dark brown skin and large, luminous black eyes. He shook Tony's hand. "I was just headed toward the gym," Manny said, stroking a large, drooping mustache. "Care to come along?"

"No, I wouldn't," said Tony, panicking. "Couldn't we talk over a couple of bottles? I

want you to come to Brazil with me. I've got
the route all planned."

Manny looked him up and down. "You've
gotten soft since you left the service, Tony. I've
seen it happen before. Men give up the discipline of years and they fall to pieces. It happens
very fast. In a few years you'll have a paunch
and be puffing and wheezing just to catch the
bus—you'll see. You're simply asking for a
heart attack."

"Would you like to throw dirt on me now,
and get it over with?"

"Come on," Manny said. "I've got to do my
workout. An hour a day keeps the doctor
away." He picked up an athletic bag and swung
it over his shoulder. "Bring that," he said,
pointing to a leather pouch on the table.

It was very heavy. Tony opened it and looked
inside. He saw a large, black Browning auto-
matic.

"Hell," he said.

"There are people out there who want to kill
me—from the government of Guyana to the
lowliest nut. Just last week some drug-crazed
lunatic came up to me and said he'd wanted to
shoot me for years but his psychiatrist had
talked him out of it. 'Thanks,' I said. 'Great
news. Just let me know if you change your
mind.'" He shook his head in disbelief. "It's
a jungle out there. Tell me about your plans on
the way over."

At the gym, Manny changed into shorts,
socks, and gym shoes. Tony followed him into
the gym, watching as he hoisted himself up and

down between the parallel bars and kissed his knees. Manny nodded toward the young men sweating on wall bars and lifting weights. "They can't do this. I'm forty-three. But they just don't have the strength and the flexibility. Every day I concentrate on a different set of muscles. If I throw a rope to a man who is drowning in a rapid, I *must* be strong enough to pull him to the bank."

"What about the route?" Tony asked, trying not to sound impatient. "Will you come with us?"

Manny dropped gracefully to the ground. "It is a ridiculous plan," he said cheerfully. "But I like you, Tony. You are a good man. And it has been many years since I've been in that area." He grinned broadly. "I will go!" He grabbed Tony's hand and shook it. Then he grabbed Tony and hugged him. Tony felt several ribs creak in protest.

"Now," Manny said, "we will go to my apartment to celebrate. Also, I have low-level radar and high-level NASA infrared satellite maps of the area. That part of the world is a small obsession of mine."

Manny's apartment was chaotic. Books and papers lay everywhere. One wall was obscured by a map-drawer cabinet and files for photographs. Shelves were lined with Mayan artifacts. Manny ushered Tony into another room with steel cabinets containing a Sten gun, a Hasselblad, a combined .22 rifle and .410 shotgun, a 12-bore shotgun, a Linhof panoramic, a 16-bore shotgun, and a pair of Olympuses and a case of lenses. On the floor stood a large radio transmitter. On a spare table various pieces of a knife were spread about and a set of plans for it that looked like a diagram from an IQ test.

"This is the Brewer Explorer Survival Knife," said Manny, taking a complete model out of a drawer. "It has a 6¼-inch stainless steel blade, a saw, a clinometer for calculating the height of mountains, and a six-centimeter ruler. This small hole in the blade is for sighting when you use it as a signaling reflector; this large rectangular hole converts it into wire cutters. It can also be made into a harpoon. This end cap screws off like this and, inside the hollow handle there's a compass and a waterproof container with the Morse code printed on its sides. It holds a nylon fishing line, two sewing needles, one float, two lead sinkers, an exacto blade, three matches, a flint stick, and a suture needle with suture material attached."

Manny's voice was excited. "We will each need one of these. It's good for skinning alligators. We will need many stores and we will hire Indians to help us. We will pay them eight dollars a day except for the cook—we will pay him ten."

He paused for breath. "Ah, Tony, these will be good times for you and me. Are you hungry? I will heat up a pizza!"

Tony groaned. "You and Chris should get along well—she thinks pizza is the food of the gods." Manny looked at him sharply. "She? This is getting more interesting all the time."

* * *

As they were eating, Manny said "Tell me more about this Chris—why is she funding the expedition?"

"Chris is short for Christine," Tony answered. "She's Percy Fawcett's granddaughter. Also, she's not just funding this little jaunt. She's coming with us."

Manny's eyes widened. "A woman?" He sat back in his chair. "What is your connection with her?"

"We're lovers, Manny."

Manny shook his head back and forth slowly. "I don't like this, Tony. This is dangerous territory, not a cruise for tourists. People go into the jungles and never come out again. We are used to these hardships, but has she any experience with these things?"

"She's an urban creature, Manny. But she's determined to do this. I think she feels like her life has no shape to it, no edge. It's more a quest for her than an expedition."

"Perhaps you could suggest she go to an ashram in India, or else one of these adventure tours where you hike and sleep in a tent?"

"She doesn't take kindly to condescension. This is important to her. She's been floundering for a long time and I don't want to deny her this chance."

"Nor deny it to yourself," Manny answered. "I have seen you trying to force yourself into this civilized world. You should not try it, Tony. Ever since you left the service, you've been like a lost soul." He sighed. "Well, there is precedent, of course, for the woman. Isabella Bird, Mary Kingsley, Alexandra David-Neel were all untried women who became excellent explorers. Do you vouch for her?''

"She'll work out. I've a lot of faith in Chris. If I thought she couldn't make it, I would have told her so.''

"You will be responsible for her, Tony.''

"I'm responsible for us all.''

That evening, Lily waded desolately through the hordes at her friend Nan's party. Her hostess came up to her and put a martini into her hand. "For heaven's sakes, Lily, you look like Cassandra prophesying the fall of Troy. Whatever is the trouble? And where's your charming daughter?''

"She's packing,'' Lily said, dabbing at her eyes with a handkerchief. "She's going to Brazil.''

"Really? Christine never struck me as the beach-and-bikini type. She's too short-waisted to look good in those swimsuits.''

"You don't understand,'' Lily wailed. "She's going on some sort of harebrained expedition to trace Percy's steps on his last trip.''

"The one he never came back from?'' Nan asked, raising her eyebrows. "Whatever for? And aren't there bugs in those jungles?''

"How should I know why? I'm only her mother, after all. She was babbling about Percy, and the changes since he went there, and the way the world is closing in on us, and all sorts of rubbish.''

"Excuse me,'' a short, rather stout man said, tapping Nan on the shoulder. "You haven't introduced me to this lovely lady, Nan. How could you be so remiss?''

"Hello, Tommy. Lily, this is Thomas Farragut. He writes all those detestable articles for the *London Sun*—the ones no other ever admits to reading but does. He's quite unscrupulous, so watch what you say. I invite him to see what sort of lies he'll make up about me and put in his paper. He always depicts my parties so surrealistically. Anyways, I must look after the rest of these people. I'm quite certain I never invited all of them.'' She wandered off aimlessly into the crowd.

Tommy waited until Nan was safely out of earshot. "Dear lady, did I hear you say your daughter was going to the Amazon? Is she interested in the ecology?''

Lily thought for a moment. "I suppose—I mean, everyone is, these days, aren't they?''

Mr. Farragut beamed. "Absolutely. A very hot topic. Would you like to tell me more?''

The doorbell rang insistently. Mumbling, Christine pulled a pillow over her head. "Tony, it's the door," she muttered.

"It's your house and your door. You get it.'' He rolled onto his side and under the covers. The doorbell rang again.

Blearily, Christine staggered out of bed and threw on a robe. "You're a pig,'' she called over her shoulder. She made sure to slam the bedroom door after her.

"Yes?'' she said to the two men in the hallway. One of them was middle-aged, short, stout, and rosy. The other was young, tall, and thin.

"Ms. Christine Fawcett?" said the short one cheerily.

"I think so. Go away."

He grabbed her hand. "Thomas Farragut, *London Sun.*" He flashed a press card. "Ted, take a picture." There was a flash of light. "He loves doing that," Farragut said. "My sister's boy. We're teaching him the ropes." He winked at Christine.

"What the hell is this . . ."

"Your mother, my dear, your mother. Lily and I are friends and she was telling me all about your great adventure into the Brazilian rain forest. Very exciting. Wanted me to get you some publicity. Good of her, don't you think? Can I come in?" He stepped into the apartment. "Thanks. It won't take long."

"Chris, what's going on?" Tony came into the room in his pajama bottoms which, unfortunately, he had put on backwards.

"Thomas Farragut, *London Sun.* Ted, get a picture of the gentleman." Ted did. "This dear lady was about to give me an interview about the upcoming expedition. You wouldn't be Anthony Blondell, would you? I've heard all about you from Lily." He winked at Tony.

"Oh, God," Tony said.

Christine had left the country by the time Farragut's story appeared, which was probably just as well. Because of its romance, and the fact that there was a woman involved, it generated a small amount of interest. The wire services picked it up and in papers all over the world, there were fillers about the brave lady explorer who, with her lover, was searching for her long-lost uncle and investigating conditions in the Brazilian rain forest.

3

Over the next month, Christine's excitement mounted. She began studying maps and spent a week going to various camping shops picking out equipment. With almost unerring accuracy, everything she bought was defective.

She and Tony searched through the accumulating pile of ''campaign-tested'' equipment, looking for something usable. After filling two pairs of heavy plastic water bottles and seeing them each split along the sides when the caps were screwed down, Tony had an inspiration. He went to SAS headquarters in Hereford and wielding the powerful psychological weapon of guilt, persuaded his old commander to become a ''sponsor'' of the expedition by donating equipment.

In triumph, he presented to Christine an outfit of lightweight jungle fatigues and a floppy camouflage hat covered with wire mesh fine enough to keep out blackfly. She was immediately inspired to put them on and presented herself to Tony for his approval. She felt tough and ready for anything.

Tony looked at her for a moment and said, ''You'd better start working out in the gym with me. You look like you've never lifted anything heavier than a pencil in your life.''

''I haven't.''

''We'll start tomorrow, at six.''

''What, after dinner?''

''No, love, before breakfast.''

Christine goose-stepped out of the room to change.

Every morning Christine dragged herself to the local health club and, as she put it, ''sweated like a pig.'' Tony went with her and over time, he became even leaner and possessed of a ferocious energy which she found at once reassuring and a little frightening.

''I used to have trouble picturing you in the service,'' she told him once, as he lifted weights as if he had piston rods instead of arms, ''but now I don't. You hardly seem human.'' He smiled a bit and went on with his workout.

Manny came by often to consult, to encourage, to argue. He was unfailingly courteous to Christine and managed to leave unvoiced the hesitations he had about her as a traveling companion. He had a genuine love of places remote from civilization and seemed, to Christine, to glory most in the least desirable aspects of life in those areas. He spoke about the dangers they would face the way a gourmet speaks about a particularly delicate and rare dish.

''There is, of course, amoebic and bacillary dysenteries; yellow, blackwater, and dengue fevers; malaria; cholera; typhoid; rabies; hepatitis; and tuberculosis,'' he told them with relish. Christine thought he could barely restrain himself from rubbing his hands together.

"Of course," he said disparagingly, "these are common to many parts of the world—they are nothing special. But there are some things which are very particular to the places we are going.

"There is Chagas' disease, for instance, which is produced by a protozoan and is carried by various species of assassin bugs which bite you on the face or neck and then, when they have eaten their fill, defecate next to the puncture. When you scratch the resulting itch, you rub the droppings and their cargo of protozoa into your bloodstream; between one and twenty years later you begin to die from incurable damage to the heart and brain.

"Then we have river blindness, which is transmitted by blackfly and causes worms which migrate to the eyeball; and leishmaniasis, which is a bit like leprosy and is produced by a parasite carried by sandflies." Manny shook his head. "Did you know," he asked them, "that it infects eighty percent of Brazilian troops on exercise in the jungle in rainy season?"

"How interesting," Christine said, trying to maintain a conversational tone. "Won't we be there in the rainy season?"

"Precisely," Manny answered, beaming at her as though she were a prize pupil.

"Perhaps it would be wiser to wait?" she asked.

"Oh, no," Tony and Manny chorused. "We might have to travel some very small rivers, so the rainy season is the only time that makes sense.''

"Of course," Christine said faintly.

"The bigger animals," Manny went on, "are much friendlier than you might suppose."

"I don't suppose much," Christine answered. "Just how much friendlier are they?"

"The jaguar will kill you with a bite to the head, but only in exceptional circumstances. Two vipers, the fer-de-lance, which is up to seven and a half feet long, and the bushmaster, which is up to twelve feet long, only kill you if you step on them."

"I'll try to avoid it," Christine murmured.

"The anaconda smothers you, but it only tightens its grip when you breathe out; the electric eel can only deliver six hundred forty volts before its breakfast; and the piranha only rips you to bits if you're already bleeding, and the giant catfish merely takes your feet off at the ankles if it sees you in the water." Christine wondered idly just how one knew whether an eel had breakfasted or not.

"Really it is the smaller animals which are much more annoying—the mosquitoes, blackfly, tapir-fly, chiggers, ticks, and so on. But it is the candiru," said Manny, his face lit up with admiration, "that is the most terrible of them all.

"They are tiny catfish adapted for a parasitic life in the gills of bigger fish. But if, let us say, you have too much to drink, and inadvertently urinate as you swim, any homeless candiru, attracted by the smell, will think you are a big fish, swim up the stream of uric acid, enter your urethra, and stick out a set of spines so it will not be dislodged." Manny shrugged. "There is nothing to be done, of course. The pain is spectacular. You must go to a hospital before your bladder bursts; you must ask a surgeon to cut off your penis." And he made a chopping motion with his right hand.

Christine glanced over at Tony. He looked, she noted with some gratification, rather queasy about his own gills.

After Manny had gone, she said "Your friend is completely 'round the bend. He ought to be put away. Why are we taking him?"

"He's only telling us what to expect," Tony said, sounding irritated.

"That's not what bothers me," she answered. "It's the fact that none of this unsettles him is what's frightening. I have the most horrible feeling that he thinks being devoured by something is the perfect way to end an evening."

She started to laugh. "Can you imagine the sorts of travel brochures he'd write? 'Come to the rain forest and see a place unspoiled by civilization—no cars, no phones, no penicillin. Experience firsthand disease and pestilence unseen in Europe since the Middle Ages.' He'd do a booming trade."

"He's still alive," Tony pointed out. "Manny is very fond of life, I assure you. He once told me he has every intention of dying at a ripe old age, in bed, with plenty of time to repent all his sins. And he intends to have lots of sins to repent. He's not mad at all—just a little overenthusiastic. I wouldn't have asked Manny to come if I didn't have complete confidence in him. But he's got me in a proper sweat about that candiru fish. I wonder what we'll do about that?"

Two days later, he showed Christine a little box with a hole on one end and a front panel that had been cut out and replaced with a tea strainer. "What is this?" she asked, completely baffled.

"This," he said proudly, "is an invention Manny and I cooked up. It's an anti-candiru device. Allow me to demonstrate." They practiced putting it on for several hours.

At the beginning of January, they were ready to leave. The day before they left, all three of them went out for dinner. They had brought a map that showed Percy's last trip and they went over it again closely. Christine pointed out the area the explorers were last seen and Manny nodded his head slowly.

"If we decide to go so far north, we may meet the Yanomanis who inhabit this part of the forest. They are very violent."

Christine looked at him with real exasperation. "You are always the bearer of good news." She refilled their wine glasses. "Are they cannibals or headhunters or real-estate developers?"

"Some anthropologists believe they were the first people to reach South America from the north," Manny answered. "They have very fair skins, and green eyes sometimes. They are the largest untouched group of Indians left in the rain forest. The other Indians are terrified of them.

"Basically, they are hunter-gatherers and there's not much food in these forests. When times are hard, they kill the newborn girls, so there are never enough women to go around and they fight over them. Within their own groups, in formalized duels, they hit each other over the head with ten-foot-long clubs. Outside their group, they raid other settlements for women and kill the enemy men with six-foot-long arrows tipped with curare. And on top of that, they've no concept of natural death, so if anyone dies from a fever, it's the result of evil magic worked by an enemy shaman. Each death must be avenged."

"Does this sort of thing still go on?" Tony asked.

"They are killing each other," Manny said, "right now." All three of them exchanged glances and then each grabbed his wine glass, downing the contents in a gulp.

"To the expedition," Christine said, holding her empty glass high.

After a tearful last evening together, Christine told her mother not to come to the airport to see them off. She didn't think she could stand another farewell.

Lily had taken it into her head that it was Tony's fault Christine was going. No amount of argument could persuade her differently. She had begun to call him "that adventurer" and said several times that there were worse things in the world than being a socialist.

Sitting in the airport waiting room, drinking abominable coffee, Christine wondered if this was really happening to her. It wasn't possible that a person could simply wake up one morning, shower, eat breakfast, take a taxi to Heathrow, get on a plane, and then disappear into the Amazon rain forest. How could the sum of these mundane actions be so quixotic and unimaginable?

After they boarded the plane, Christine looked around for some clue that her past life was vanishing. There was nothing. The interior of the plane was as ordinary as one would expect. The stewardesses could have worked for any airline. The packages of peanuts were vile.

Tony glanced over at her as she fussed with her seatbelt. "You've been awfully quiet today. Is anything wrong?"

"I suppose I'm missing a sense of drama. Surely going off on an expedition for four months should feel differently than going off to Nice for the weekend?"

He shrugged. "Better save up your adrenalin. You'll need it later on. Right now, relax. Our biggest challenge for the next few weeks is going to be cutting through more bureaucratic red tape than you've ever dreamed existed. We're not going to step off the plane into the arms of a jaguar."

"Tony is correct," Manny said. "Brasilia is not a great city like Rio de Janeiro, but it is still a big city. You do not need to transform yourself so quickly. Metamorphosis is a slow process." And with that, he shut his eyes and went to sleep. Not long after, Tony did the same.

Looking at them, Christine felt lonely and out of step. The feeling of being a small child tagging along after the grown-ups was unpleasant. She settled back in her seat and closed her eyes. "When in Rome . . ." she thought.

Swooping and wheeling like a bird of prey, she felt the wind rush into her face. It was perfumed and rank. Smells and colors assaulted her. Below was a massive river, sluggish and brown. Flamingoes stood in it in pink clumps, their necks bent in graceful curves. When they saw her, they exploded upward, surrounding her in rosy clouds. With harsh screams they departed as quickly as they had gathered.

In surprise she saw that she had changed. Bronze feathers covered her and instead of hands she had talons that gleamed like gold. Her vision was uncompromisingly clear and as limitless as the landscape she inhabited.

She circled a mountain, marveling at the complex geometry. Pleats of stone receded in shadow while outcroppings caught the sunlight. Green lichen faded into brown rock and the crown was capped with snow.

"This is paradise," she thought. "Unconstrained freedom and sensuality without guilt . . . I've been reborn and my new shape embodies all that I now am." With a cry of pleasure she dived into a canyon, watching the rocky walls rush by her. She was thirsty and would drink some Coca-Cola. . . .

"Chris . . . do you want some cola to drink?" Tony asked her, jogging her arm.

She opened her eyes to see a stewardess

leaning toward her with a plastic cup. "Oh, yes, thank you," she said, taking the glass. "Was I asleep?" She sipped at the drink.

"I suppose you must have dozed off." He looked at her. "Are you all right, sweetheart? You look like you've lost your best friend."

"I was dreaming." Christine blinked sleepily and stared out the window. They were flying in the clouds. She could see nothing but white. "It's not at all like the real thing," she murmured.

"I'm sure the Pepsi company will be glad to hear that," Tony said.

She looked at him. "What *are* you talking about?"

Three weeks later, sitting in a bar in Cuiaba, Christine decided they had found their way, not to Brazil, but to some small neighborhood of Hell.

"This is the Circle of Bureaucrats," she told Tony, downing her third beer. "Dante didn't talk about it because it's relatively new. It's not even a circle, really; it's a suburb next to a roundabout and it's where they send all the paper pushers, bean counters, officious, petty, small-minded . . ."

"Now, Chris, it isn't as bad as all that," Tony said soothingly.

"Stop being so patronizing," she snapped. "It certainly is as bad as all that, and you know it. I heard you telling Manny you were going to shove those permits up . . ."

"Yes, well, I suppose it has been a bit grim."

"Brasilia was the worst city I've ever seen.

No one wants to live there. And don't try to tell me I'm prejudiced. Anyone with any money gets out of it as soon as the weekend comes, and there's no point in trying to get anything done on a Monday because they're too pissed off about being back to listen to you. All they want to do is make accusations about your intentions so they can vent a little spleen. I've been accused of being a spy, a gold prospector, and a whore, all at the same time."

"I admit that it has been a bit unpleasant, and I'm no good at this sort of negotiation. Thank God Manny's here. At least he knows whom to bribe."

"Where is he, anyway?"

"He's off greasing more wheels. If we can get these last permissions, we'll be allowed into the interior. I think he's taking some sort of subminister of the Department of the Redundancy Department out for dinner."

"The man's a saint," Christine said, with true fervor. "I don't think I could have stood another evening with one of these chaps. Where is there to eat in Cuiaba, anyway? The place is dull as ditch water."

"It's called *O Regionalissimo*. It's the best restaurant here, for whatever that's worth. Manny didn't ask us because he knew how disgusted we were feeling."

"Are *we* going to eat tonight?"

Tony shrugged. "Why bother?" he asked. "Another round," he called to the waiter. "At least they know all the important English words," he said.

* * *

Christine woke early in the shack that served as a research station for various Brazilian scientific expeditions. She had been disturbed by a high-pitched, metallic chattering that came from a corner of the roof.

Lying in her hammock, she switched on a torch and saw three very black, very furry bats hanging from the walls. They moved crabwise up to the corrugated iron ceiling and disappeared through a crack.

Deciding that it was foolish to sleep anymore, she lifted the mosquito netting and swung out of bed. She stepped on a toad that had huddled up to her backpack. It croaked and hopped under a tarpaulin.

Uncertain whether to scream or laugh, Christine decided to be silently thankful that her mother wasn't here to see any of this. She moved into the storeroom that also served as a kitchen to make coffee and breakfast. At once, plates jumped into each other, pots banged, and packets of rice swung on their chain hangings.

She briefly considered the possibility of poltergeists but dismissed it as foolish. The torch revealed the brown backs and white stomachs of the rats that scurried out of her way to their nests concealed among the boxes and pieces of equipment on the concrete floor.

As she opened tins of oats, sugar, and powdered milk to make porridge, she reflected on the past weeks that had taken her so far from her home and everything familiar and comfortable. Somehow, it seemed as if she had always been here, in this village on the banks of the

Culuene River, with its wide, grassy streets, whitewashed bungalows, and wattle and daub huts. London had faded to a dream, the irritations of Brazilian officialdom were over, and the only compelling reality was this place and the mysteries that lay hidden in the rain forest that loomed beyond.

This town was the last they would see of civilization for months. It hovered on the edge of the forest, a last defiant testament to technology and the twentieth century. Now all that was necessary was assembling the crew that would help them on their journey and signing the final sheet of permissions. With these, they would step into a world indifferent to their whims and barely touched by human constructs. It would be a place where permits and official stamps carried no weight.

Outside, it was almost light. A lizard rustled away over the leaves beneath the orange trees. The town generator and river-pumping motor spluttered into life. An officer shouted orders to his soldiers, and the family in the bungalow opposite turned on their radio. It blared across the town and she heard Tony and Manny stirring.

"Morning," Tony mumbled. He poured out coffee for all of them and sat on a crate, staring blankly at the wall. "I'll never get used to that racket," he complained. "You'd think that peace and quiet would be the one thing you could count on out here, but we haven't been able to escape that noise since we got to Brazil."

"It is everywhere," Manny said. "In some of

the most backward of places I have been as-
sailed by the noise of the radio. It is rarely possible to escape all of civilization's inroads. The
world is a smaller place all the time.''

''Do you think the crew will show up?''
Christine asked.

''They will be here,'' Manny said confi-
dently. ''We will get our crew and we will go
on our journey and come back to great acclaim
and notoriety.''

''Hear, hear,'' Tony said, raising his coffee
mug in a salute.

''I think I'll make an inventory of the stores,''
Christine said thoughtfully. ''I'd like to be
ready to leave as soon as possible.'' She scraped
the last bit of porridge from her bowl. ''We
need to keep track of everything. Why don't
you two go and check up on the crew and get
the permissions we need to leave.''

She got up and began making a pile of cans
and sacks, sorting out what was theirs from
what had been left by previous expeditions.
She gave each of the waterproof tins a number,
then opened them and wrote down their contents. Inside, she found coffee, salt, flour, manioc, cooking oil, brown sugar, spaghetti, lentils,
dried onions, rice, and black beans. She felt the
work she was doing was important and she was
absorbed and happy.

Manny and Tony walked through the village
toward the Guardia's home. Some women,
standing chatting in a doorway, watched them
as they passed. One of them whispered something to the others and they broke out into giggles. Manny grinned at them and shouted

something in their own dialect. The women laughed again and, with a swirl of brightly colored skirts, vanished into the hut.

"What did you say to them?" Tony asked.

"I was merely telling them how lovely they were," Manny said. He was craning his neck, trying to see into the house.

"Is that the censored version, Manny?"

"It is translated to conform with your English morals."

"Please, Manny, don't start any trouble. The last thing we need is to offend the entire village."

"I have done nothing, my friend. You worry too much. Never have I jeopardized an expedition by any indiscreet behavior. And you are very unfair, also. You are here with your lady, yet you begrudge me even an admiring glance. It is selfish of you."

"Looking is all I do these days," Tony said. "Sleeping in those hammocks is enough of a challenge. Anything more energetic seems like asking for a broken neck. Not to mention that I feel like I should wear armor at night. Those insects are the very devil, netting or no."

"But as you see," Manny said, "the human spirit is a brave and adaptable one or else this would be an empty place. Love conquers all, as they say. Mosquitoes cannot stifle passion forever."

"I'll take your word for it," Tony said, scratching at the back of his neck. "There's the Guardia's house. Let's get this paperwork straightened out."

Tables and benches were arranged outside

the hut under a stand of lemon trees. Groups
of men were drinking and playing dominoes.
Inside, Mariano, the Guardia, greeted them. He
had quick, intelligent eyes and a warm smile.
Tony's own heart warmed in response to Mariano's greeting. Perhaps everything would go
smoothly.

Three walls of the hut were covered with
family pictures, a portrait of the Pope, and plastic dolls. The entire far end of the room, however, was devoted to Bare artifacts, for Mariano
was a Bare Indian and proud of his heritage.
He showed them manioc graters with pebbles
set into the surface in intricate patterns; baskets
covered in simple black-dyed geometrical de-
signs; blow pipes and dart pouches of different
sizes; curare pouches; bows and arrows; and
necklaces of jaguar teeth.

Sitting over the coffee his wife served them
in tiny blue cups, they discussed their journey.
Mariano brought out a map, and watched as
Manny's calloused thumb traced out the route,
from a tributary of the Culuene, over to the Rio
dos Mortes, across the Serro do Roncandor, and
then along the great Rio Araguaya.

"Percy Fawcett was looking for a lost city,"
Tony said. "He was convinced there was a lost
world somewhere in the rain forest."

"And do you look for these things, too? Do
you search for wealth and ancient relics?" Mariano asked, looking at him shrewdly.

"Of course not," Tony said. "But the sponsor of our expedition is his granddaughter, and
she wants to retrace his route. She'd like to

write a book documenting the changes in the area since 1925."

"There are many," Mariano answered. "Your Percy Fawcett would be dismayed, I think. Do you have your permissions from FUNAI?" he asked, referring to the government agency whose charter was to protect the various Indian tribes.

Manny showed the sheaf of papers that attested to his ability to speak Portuguese, his knowledge of Brazilian law, the vaccination certificates and X rays of everyone, the expedition's proposal and route, and the stamps and signatures of a dozen ministry officials, professors, and museum directors.

Mariano examined them all carefully. "You are going to Xingu Park here in the Matto Grosso, but you also may travel to Yanomani Park in Roraima." He rubbed his chin thoughtfully. "You must be careful. In all honesty, gentlemen, what happens to you is your own affair, and if you are killed or not means little to me. But it's bad for the Indians if they kill you. It's bad for public opinion. I care about that very much."

"We'll keep it in mind," Manny assured him and with a flourish, Mariano signed the last piece of paper. "You must speak to Señor Raeder about your crew," he said. "I have nothing to do with that."

"Who is this Raeder?" Tony asked.

"An Argentinian. He arranges these things— he is good with Europeans and makes sure they do not make the Indians drunk. He is a bit out of place here, but in this part of the world, a man's past is his own affair."

"Where do we find him?"

Mariano shrugged. "His hut is over there, but he is not in it. I am sure he is around someplace. After all, where is there to go?" And with a final wish for a fruitful journey, he ushered them from his home.

They returned in a jubilant mood, Manny waving the signed paper over his head and doing an impromptu jig. Nearing their hut, they saw Christine standing in the doorway. She was shouting at a stranger.

"That's not acceptable, Mr. Raeder. I don't care what your qualifications are, what languages you speak, or how well you know the area. You are not the crew we contracted for, you are not going to be the crew we contracted for, and that is all I have to say. Good day." She stood there with her arms folded, glowering at the man.

"What's all this, Chris?" Tony asked.

"He says he's our cook and boatman," Christine answered.

"Rudolf Raeder, at your service," the stranger said. He was a tall, thin man, with a long, rather mournful face. He looked to be in his late forties. There were bags under his eyes, and hard lines running from his chin to his mouth. His linen suit was clean but frayed around the cuffs. To Tony, he looked very much like a man who had fallen onto hard times.

"I have explained to the young lady," he said in English that bore only a trace of an accent, "that, due to circumstances, it is impossible to hire any crew at the moment. Therefore, I offer my services. I am very knowledgeable in the waters around the Rio dos Mortes. You will find me an excellent navigator and a respectable cook.''

"What happened to the Indian crew that was supposed to be waiting for us?" Tony demanded.

"Alas, but there are none available. Most of the young men have gone off to the larger cities to find work in the factories. The others are already engaged. This is now mainly a town of women and old men. I have been unable to hire anyone reliable. Many expeditions have set out using my men, but my business is not what it was. I deeply regret any inconvenience and, of course, I offer my services, at no extra pay.''

"Why should we pay you extra?" Manny muttered. "Your white skin is no asset here.''

"Of course," Mr. Raeder said, bowing his head slightly. "But, unless any of you know the many tributaries and swamps of the river, I suggest you do not disdain my services. People have been lost for months in the backwaters. Many have not returned.''

"Wait here," Tony said, then motioned Christine and Manny aside. "What do you think?" he asked them.

"I don't trust him," Christine said flatly. "How do we know he's what he claims? And besides, he gives me a bad feeling. I can't put my finger on it, but there's something shifty about him.''

Tony turned to Manny. "What do you say?"

"We must take a boatman. What he says

about the backwaters is true. Even skilled pilots
can get lost and I am not extremely knowledg-
able in these waters. There is much that does
not appear on the maps. To go without a local
guide is suicidal. Mariano said nothing to his
detriment.''

Tony looked at Christine again. "You're the
leader, Tony," she said. "I'll live with whatever you decide. There's nothing concrete
against him, it's true."

Tony walked over to Raeder and said, "What
brings an Argentinian to this out of the way
place? No offense, but you seem to have fallen
on rather hard times."

"You are correct. Before the Falklands war, I
was a prosperous man. But in the aftermath, and
with the chaos in the Argentinian economy, I am
afraid I am greatly reduced in circumstances."

"And why did you leave your own country?"

Raeder shrugged. "Fortune is a fickle mistress. She spins her wheel and those who were
once on top are now on the bottom."

"Got on the wrong side of the military, did
you?"

Raeder smiled. "You are an astute man,
Mr . . . ?"

"Blondell . . . Mark Anthony Blondell. And
this is Manuel Aburto and Christine Fawcett."

Raeder bowed to Christine and shook hands
with the men. "Pardon me," he said to Christine, "but I could not help but wonder if you
are related to Percy Fawcett?"

"He was my grandfather. We're going to retrace his route and complete it."

"And perhaps find the lost city for which he searched?" Raeder said, laughing.

"I think the Arthur Conan Doyle aspects have been put aside," Christine said dryly.

"Of course. It was just my little joke." He looked expectantly at them. "So, shall I be included on the expedition? I should very much like to come!"

"You're on," Tony said, and shook Raeder's hand.

4

The next day, their journey began. As they sailed upriver, Christine turned to watch the village disappear and the jungle close in behind them. Sunlight, filtered through the endless, broad-leaved canopy, became flat and lifeless. The air was moist and humid, and smelled slightly sweet. She felt as a physical weight the vastness of the forest, its indifference, and its suggestion of something vague and uncontrollable hidden in the lush growth that surrounded them. She tried to swallow down the panic that rose inside her.

Seeing her fear, Manny said, "The jungle is a disconcerting place. I have seen grown men cry like babies after only a few weeks. Once, when I was lost in the Venezuelan rain forest, I became so terrified I panicked and ran. It seemed like my soul was being smothered. I remember how the vines slapped my face and the roots tangled my feet. I would have given my life's blood for a clearing and a sight of the sky."

Christine smiled slightly. "I thought it was just me. I feel claustrophobic."

"Oh no, it is the same for everyone who was not born here. To know the jungle is to know fear."

"Right," Tony said. "Manny's correct. And there are a few rules we're going to follow while we're in here, to try and make life more bearable. When I was at Hereford, I talked to Major Essex who spent time in Borneo. He gave me some tips and we'll follow them.

"First, we've not many clothes, so each of us will keep one dry set in a sealed bag. Get into those at night after you've eaten. Powder yourself all over with zinc talc—don't feel shy about it. We have to avoid rashes and skin fungus. Then go to sleep. When you wake, you'll wear the wet clothes."

He saw Christine squirm a bit. "I know it's uncomfortable, but don't weaken. If you do, you'll have two sets of wet clothes in no time. You'll lose sleep and lose strength and we'll be in for real trouble.

"Try to keep as many pairs of dry socks as you can. Seal them up and stuff them in every spare cranny you can find in your pack. Each morning, soak the pair you're going to wear in insect repellant, to keep leeches out of your boots. Rub it on your arms and round your waist and neck and in your hair, too, but not on your forehead because the sweat carries it into your eyes and it stings. At night, cover yourself against mosquitoes. Take them seriously because malaria is a terrible thing and it's easy to get, pills or no.

"Also, no more shaving. It's too easy for a

nick to turn septic out here. One of the fellows
told me the only part of him he could keep clean
was his teeth and that brushing them was the
high spot of his day.

"We'll take it easy at first, but I want us all
to be acclimatized by the time we have to cross
over to the Rio dos Mortes. That trek will probably be the hardest thing we do." He looked
about him. "Are there any questions?" Everyone was silent.

"Good. Then, to make it official, here's our
list of assigned duties: Christine, you'll keep
track of supplies, foodstuffs, motor oil, cartridges . . . everything. Raeder is the cook and
navigator. Manny will help with the piloting
and he and I will try to do some hunting and
fishing so we can get some variety in our diet.

"Our worst dangers on this trip are disease
and discomfort. Let's try to avoid them both.
And remember, we all rely on each other. Each
member is important. No matter how much we
get on each other's nerves, try to keep that in
mind." He paused for breath, then said, "End
of lecture."

Manny and Christine applauded. "Alan
Quartermain couldn't have done it better, darling," she said. Tony bowed his head in ac-
knowledgment. Manny took off his Cleveland
Indians' baseball cap and tipped it in respect.

Soon after, the river began to turn and twist,
the banks behind appearing to merge together
into a single impenetrable thicket, shutting
them off from retreat. They pushed past islets

and mysterious tributaries, and saw piles of driftwood planed and polished by the rush of floodwaters.

A monitor lizard, perched on one such pile, reared up on its hind legs to watch them and then scuttled away between the broken branches.

"What do those lizards taste like?" Tony asked.

"Like shit," Manny answered. "And their meat smells like a burst abscess."

"Hardly sounds like the appropriate stuff for our four-star cuisine, does it?" Tony said to Christine.

"I'll take the tinned beef," she answered.

A kite, flying low enough for them to hear the rush of air through its wings, circled overhead for a bit, then soared away, mewing its shrill cry.

They began to encounter rapids and the farther upstream they went, the more turbulent and numerous they became. At each one, Raeder drove the canoe for the central cascade of the current while Manny and Tony, their back muscles bunched, poled the bow to the left or right of each oncoming rock. Heavy waves crashed over and into the boat and they were drenched.

"This is wonderful," Christine thought, as a wave knocked her onto her back. "It's like an amusement park. When things settle down a bit, I'll get Tony to show me how to use those poles. I wonder if I'm going to drown?"

Late in the afternoon, they came to a wider stretch of river. Tony decided to make camp.

"We'll have good fishing here," Manny said, looking at the swirling white water, the fallen trees, and the eddies by the far bank.

They pulled the canoe well out of the water and tied its bow rope high up the trunk of a tree, in case of floods in the night. As they stretched out for a rest, butterflies began to gather. Hundreds of them flying at different heights and speeds—floating, fluttering, flying fast and direct, gliding—they settled on all of them, clustering on their shirts, and sucking the sweat from their arms.

"It's a dream," Christine thought. "It's like being buried in flower petals." The butterflies clung to her, their wings quivering as they fed. She crawled slowly toward the canoe to get her camera. Disturbed, they rose in a cloud and swirled around her, dipping and hovering, waiting for a chance to land again. Lying on her stomach, Christine took picture after picture of a world clothed in the iridescent wings of butterflies.

Reluctantly, the men got to their feet. The butterflies moved upward into the canopy of leaves, and flew away. "Let's make camp," Tony said. "We'll have to clear a space for a shelter, so dig out the machetes."

They cut down saplings and bushes between the taller trees and cleared a patch of ground. Manny tugged at a coil of vine and cut it into lengths. Then he and Tony made cross-poles from which to sling the hammocks and mosquito netting.

Christine stepped back to look at it and

laughed. "It reminds me of the house the Lost Boys and Peter Pan built for Wendy. But it needs a roof."

"No problem," Tony said. He took the big tarpaulin from the canoe and spread it over the poles, then stuck sticks up underneath to maintain the pitch and to stop water from gathering in sagging pools over their heads.

He stepped back to survey his work. "Your dream house in Never-never Land," he said, bowing to her. "It's not exactly Christopher Wren, but it'll do."

"It's lovely," Christine said, "and not a pirate in sight. Although I assume there are crocodiles lurking about."

"Complete with alarm clocks," Tony said, rummaging through the packs, looking for the fishing lines. "Do you think fish like Spam?"

"I can't imagine anything liking Spam, but it's worth a try. I'm certainly willing to risk a piece if it means eating fresh fish," Christine answered.

"You're a noble, self-sacrificing woman, Chris."

He opened a can and starting jabbing pieces onto the hooks. "Care to try your hand?" he asked her.

"Certainly. What are we trying to catch?"

"Anything."

All four of them took a line and tossed it out just beyond the immediate eddies by the bank. Almost at once, Christine's line grew taut. Quickly she hauled it in. There was a flash of dark blue and silver, and a fish about fifteen inches long, with red-ringed eyes was thrashing on the rock. It made a curious half-hissing, half-screaming noise.

"Get back," Manny said. "It'll take your fingers off." Raeder hit the fish hard on the head with the back of his machete. Its tail flapped a tattoo on the stone, and then it lay still.

Tony bent over it. "Chris, it's a piranha. I never realized how big they were."

"It looks like something out of *Jaws*. Are we actually going to eat it?" She peered at it in disbelief. "That's the ugliest thing I've ever seen."

"We will eat it," said Raeder. "I will make a stew."

"Out of one fish?"

"There will be plenty more. They travel in schools." He opened the fish's mouth and pulled out the hook. Large, flat, triangular teeth with very sharp points stuck up from the center of the lower jaw, decreasing progressively in size to either side. He shut the mouth again, pulling back the lips to expose the teeth. The opposing triangles in the upper and lower jaws fit together perfectly.

"They cut as clean as my razor," he said. He took a clasp knife from his pocket, slit the piranha's silver belly, and pulled out a handful of guts. Then he hacked off the head and stuck it back on the fishhook. Soon they were catching piranhas with every throw.

When they had about twenty-five, they stopped. Raeder took five for the stew and Manny built a slatted table of saplings over a slow fire—a smoking rack for the rest.

After dark, they sat around the fire carefully sucking the white flesh off the sharp, tiny bones. "It's rather like eating a hairbrush," Christine thought.

"I hope the meal is satisfactory?" Raeder asked.

"Oh, yes," she said brightly.

Manny was rummaging in his pack. "We need dessert to round it off." He pulled out something that was wrapped in a pair of undershorts. Carefully, he unrolled the bundle and revealed a bottle of rum. "Baba au rhum, without the baba," he said. "I am on a diet." He poured a generous tot into everyone's mug, then downed his own portion in a single gulp.

"My God," Tony said admiringly.

Christine felt warm and cheerful. "This is much better than the Guides," she said happily. She took another swig.

"How would you know? You were never in the Guides," Tony challenged.

"Oh no? I was in it for six months." She gave him a look of immense dignity. "How would you know what I would know? You don't know everything about me, you know."

"Say that again. I dare you." He held out his cup for more rum.

"I can't remember it." She paused. "How's this? Peter Piper packed a pick . . . no, wait . . ."

Manny stood up. "Peter Piper pickled peckers . . ."

Christine giggled, then inhaled rum up her nose and started choking. Tony pounded her back.

"I'm fine," she gasped. "I just need another drink."

"We all need another drink," Manny said. He filled the mugs again, then tipped his throat back and drained the bottle. "Excellent," he said. He gave a massive belch.

Christine applauded. "Bravo."

"We should toast to the expedition," Raeder said.

"We've done that once before we left," said Tony, "but there's certainly no reason we couldn't do it again."

"And again and again and again," Christine added.

"To the Fawcett expedition," Tony said, holding his mug high.

"To fame and riches," said Raeder.

And Christine said, "God bless us everyone."

It was time for bed. They washed their mess kits in the river and kicked out the fire. Retiring modestly behind a tree, Christine turned on her torch, slung her wet clothes on a tree, toweled herself down, and searched her pack for dry clothes. Every nook and cranny in the bag was alive with inch-long ants.

With gritted teeth, she brushed off the first wave that was making exploratory maneuvers onto her arm. Looking up, she saw a regular procession climbing up the tree to stake out a claim in her wet clothes. Hastily, she pulled a plastic bag from the pack and started shoving her wet clothes into it.

As she grabbed her shirt, her arm felt as though it were being squeezed in a thousand tiny vises. Elephant ants, with massive pincers, were suspended from her hand to her elbow. The troops had arrived. She yanked them off, giving a little squeak of pain with every tug. She was gratified to hear yelps also coming from the men. It was good to know the ants had no bias.

She returned to camp with as much calm as she could muster and slipped under her mosquito net. The SAS hammock was like a tube and though it forced her to lie straight as a stick, it seemed luxuriously comfortable. The ants, swarming along the poles, rearing on their back legs to look for an entry, and the mosquitoes, whining and singing in the darkness outside, could not get in.

"Screw you," she said contentedly and closed her eyes. She was blissfully sleepy.

"Eeeeee—ai—yack yack yack yack!" something screamed in her ear, with brain-shredding force.

"Eeeeee—ai—yack yack yack yack te yooo!" responded a dissenter on the opposite side.

"Shut up!" Christine shouted.

"Wah wah wah wah!" countered four thousand frogs.

"Stop it at once," Tony yelled.

The river grew louder. Insects joined in a stereophonic version of "The Hallelujah Chorus." Something hooted. Something screamed in earnest. Something shuffled and snuffled around the discarded rice and fish bits flung in a bush.

"It's a jaguar," Christine thought. "Or an eel that's missed its breakfast. Or a snake."

"Everyone is all right?" Manny called out.

"Just wonderful," Tony answered. "There's nothing like getting away from it all. This place is noisier than Picadilly Circus on a Friday night."

"You will soon become used to it," Manny said cheerfully. "And how is Christine?"

"Oh, couldn't be better," she called back gaily. She stared down the length of her body, encased in green camouflage and started to laugh.

"You sound like a hyena," Tony muttered. "What's so funny?"

"I was just thinking of a song I once heard on the radio. Harry Secombe sang it on one of the Goon Shows."

Manny said, "Sing for us. A lullaby to put us to sleep would be most soothing."

Christine took a deep breath. "You asked for it."

> I've a great, big rock for my pillow,
> I've a bunch of grass for my bed.
> I sleep naked by the roadside,
> It's a wonder I'm not dead!
> The open road, the open road,
> The open road for meeeeee!!!

Her final word blended in nicely with the giant cicadas.

At dawn, the jungle was half obscured in a heavy morning mist. Christine placed the dry socks, pants, trousers and shirt inside two plastic bags and shook out her wet clothes. A flurry of insects discharged themselves from the trouser legs. She picked the clothes clean of all visible bugs, covered herself with antifungal powder until she looked like something that was ready for the deep fat fryer, and forced herself into the clammy outfit. She shuddered. It was a nasty start at five in the morning.

After a breakfast of fish and rice, they loaded the canoe and continued upriver. Raeder and Manny guided the boat along the twisting route. Tony lay back, scribbling in a notebook. Christine simply stared, watching the landscape slip by her.

"Are you glad you came, Chris?" Tony asked her.

She thought deeply for a moment. "Yes," she said. "I am. I can't really explain why. This place rather frightens me, the bugs are disgusting, and I hate being wet, but I'm still glad I came. How about you?"

Tony smiled. "This is the sort of thing I've always wanted to do. I feel like an animal that's been let out of its cage. I don't know if the service ever made me feel this free."

"With what branch of the military did you serve?" Raeder asked.

"SAS."

"Ah. And did you take part in the Falklands War?"

"Quite an active part."

Raeder groaned out loud. "That war ruined me. Before the war I had money, you know."

He shook his head emphatically. "Oh, yes. In my house I had two color televisions, a washer and dryer, a VCR, and a computer. I owned a Toyota. I had many possessions." He looked genuinely sad.

"It must have been hard to lose everything," Christine said sympathetically. "Did you have a house?"

"Yes. It was a big house, with two bedrooms, in Buenos Aires. Not the best neighborhood, but a good one. There was no garbage on the streets. Now, everything is gone."

"What sort of business were you in?"

"Oh, I traded. I imported and exported. I had stocks. I was a businessman. I had an office with a secretary and a fax machine." He shrugged. "So, that is the way of the world. What goes up must come down. But I shall make my fortune again. This is not the first time I have been poor. I grew up in a small village but I bettered myself. My parents left the little village and moved to Buenos Aires. We lived in the slums, in a house made of tin. There was no running water. But, as you see, I am now an educated man."

"How did you end up in that hole-in-the wall town where we found you?" Tony asked.

"When I left Argentina and came to Brazil, I worked with a travel company. We planned trips for the tourists who pay a fortune to sleep on the ground and be bitten by bugs. They are crazy. Why not sleep in a soft bed if you can afford it?

"But I am not a man who willingly works for

others. I saw the many scientists who come here to study the animals and the rain forest. All of them needed guides and cooks. Alone, they would have died. So I began a business to help them. I moved from village to village finding people. I outfitted several expeditions," he said proudly. "But, it has not been so lucrative. Always the Indians want more money. Always the scientists argue. Sometimes there is no one who will go. As you see, I must occasionally be the boss and the worker. But I am very adaptable. When I was a boy, my father and I took trips like this, looking for food. If someone will pay me to do it, then I will oblige."

"Do you think we're crazy?" Christine asked. "Like the tourists?"

Raeder turned his head toward her and smiled. "A little. Why have you left your lovely, comfortable England to come here? You do not look for gold because I have seen your equipment—you have nothing. And you say that there is nothing to find—no treasure, no wealth. No, I do not understand it. But, you are paying me and it is not my business." He shrugged again. "If it were me, I would go to Rio de Janeiro and look at the pretty girls."

Christine laughed. "You would get on famously with my mother. She gave me much the same advice."

"Mothers are very wise. It is always good to listen to them."

"But it makes for a very dull life," she objected.

"What is wrong with a dull life? I very much

enjoyed my dull life. I would like to have it
again. Besides, life is never boring if there is
enough money.''

"Why do I suddenly feel like an overprivi-
ledged Westerner with too much money and
too much time on her hands?" Christine whispered to Tony.

"Because you are one, darling." He kissed
her on the nose.

"I have not hurt your feelings I hope?" Raeder asked. He sounded distressed.

"No, not at all. I was just hit by a spasm of
liberal guilt, is all.''

Manny laughed.

"Excuse me, but I do not understand," Raeder said. "Are you ill?"

"I'll recover," she answered. "I always have
before.''

Their journey on the Culuene lasted four
more days. The river grew progressively wil-
der, and they frequently encountered rapids
and cascades. Often, they had to jump into the
river—sometimes to their waists, sometimes to
their armpits—and guide the canoe into a side
channel pushing it up the shallows, away from
the main crash of water through the central
rocks. Their boots skidded on the algae-coated
stones in the riverbed, lodging in crevices,
threatening to break off a leg at the ankle or
knee.

On their last day, they entered a wide stretch
of foaming water. The choppy waves, snatching this way and that, had ripped caves of soil

out of the banks. There was an ominous, surging noise ahead.

With the canoe pitching feverishly, they rounded a bend and the reason for the loud roar became apparent. There was a waterfall to the left of the river-course—a huge tumble of water falling over a ledge—with the way to the right blocked by thrown-up trees, piles of roots dislodged upstream, torn out in floods and tossed aside against a line of rocks here. A single small channel, a shallow rapid, looked passable. It was dangerously close to the main rush of water, but separated from the torrent by three huge boulders.

Keeping well clear of the great whirlpool beneath the waterfall, Raeder, guided between rocks by Tony's gestures, brought the boat to the base of the channel. Manny and Christine made their way carefully past them with the bow rope while Tony and Raeder held the boat steady.

Manny and Christine pulled on the rope. Tony and Raeder pushed. The boat moved up and forward some fifteen feet and then stuck. Cursing, the two men walked up the rapid, rolling small rocks aside to clear the channel. Christine and Manny waited, pulling on the rope to try and keep the canoe straight, tiring in the push of water swirling around their waists.

At last, Raeder and Tony were ready. But the channel they had made was a little to their left, a little closer to the waterfall. To pull straight, Christine and Manny had to shift their positions. Raeder motioned them to move.

Manny shifted to the right. It was only a stride, but the level of the riverbed, scooped away by the pull of the main current, suddenly dipped. He lost his footing and dropped the rope. Christine reached across to catch him, snatching at his left hand with her right. She kept the rope wrapped around her left hand.

Manny's legs thudded into hers, tangled, and then swung free into the current, weightless, as if they no longer belonged to his body. His baseball cap came off, hurtled past his shoes, spun in an eddy, and disappeared in the churning water.

Christine felt as if she were in a dream. She looked at Manny's brown hand clasped in hers. His fingers were wet and slippery. "He bites his fingernails," she thought. "I never would have guessed that. Of course, that's why they can't dig into my palm."

Manny simply looked surprised. He was feeling under the water with his free arm, trying to grip a boulder, to get a purchase on smooth, slimy rock that had been polished for centuries by tons of rolling water. To Christine, his head seemed far away as though she were seeing him through the wrong end of a telescope.

His fingers straightened, slowly edging out of hers. They moved in slow motion. Her sense of time scaled down to microseconds. Each tiny slip took centuries. His fingers slid from her fist. He turned in the current, spreadeagled. Still turning, but much faster, he was sucked under. His right ankle and shoe were bizarrely visible above the surface for a moment. Then he was lifted slightly by the water, a bundle of wet laundry, an offering to the river, and then he was gone.

"Hold the boat, Chris, hold the boat," Tony yelled.

Manny's head was visible again, sweeping round in the whirlpool, spinning, bobbing up and down in the foaming water, each orbit of current carrying him within inches of the black rocks at its edge.

Tony jumped into the boat, clambered onto the raised outboard motor frame, squatted, and then, with a cry, launched himself in a great curving leap into the center of the pool. He disappeared, surfaced, shook his head clear, spotted Manny, dived again, and caught him. Holding his head above water, he made a circuit of the whirlpool until, reaching a current that lead downstream, he thrust out like a turtle, edging yard by yard towards the bank.

Raeder got to Christine and helped her coax the boat to a strip of land. They ran down to Manny and Tony. Manny was sitting on a boulder. Tony sat beside him, an arm around his shoulders.

"You'll be all right soon," Tony said. "My very good friend, soon you'll be fine. I wouldn't let you die."

Manny, bedraggled and looking very sick, was hyperventilating, taking in great gulps of air, his body shaking. Suddenly he bent over and vomited. A thin stream of brown water dribbled out of his mouth.

"I've got your hat," Raeder said. He pulled

from his pocket Manny's cloth cap, dripping wet and shapeless. "It went right by me."

Manny looked up, smiled, and stopped his terrible spasms of breathing. Suddenly, it all seemed hilariously funny. "He saved the hat!" Christine said. She grabbed it and stuck it on Manny's head. They all laughed and laughed, rolling around on the bank.

Gasping and holding her sides, Christine thought, "So this is what it means to have hysterics. I hope I never experience it again!"

Tony decided they would go no farther that day. Finding a plateau above flood level, he and Raeder built the pole hut and pole beds. Feeling vulnerable and a little queasy, Tony took a handful of vitamin pills. Then he forced everyone else to take some too.

He stripped, took a bar of soap and went for a swim, lathering himself until he was covered in suds. Then he dried himself off, doused himself in insect repellant, dressed in clean clothes, refilled the water bottles from the river and dosed each with water-purifying pills. Still restless, he wandered about straightening out the hammocks and mosquito netting.

Feeling lonely and unsatisfied, he sat down beside Christine. "What are you doing?"

"Trying to make some notes about what we've done." She looked at him keenly. "Are you all right?"

"Yes, why?"

"That was a pretty bad scare we all had. You were wonderful, though. Of course, for a minute, I thought I'd lost you both." She put down her notebook and hugged him hard. "I don't even want to think about it."

He kissed her. "Don't you worry about me. I'm a tough old thing. You get on with your diary."

He sat there with his arm around her, simply listening to the sounds of the jungle. Then he looked over at Manny. He tried to imagine what it would mean if Manny were dead. If he hadn't pulled Manny out, thousands of brightly colored little fish would be nibbling at him right now, ingesting the tissues which taken as a whole meant Manny. All his knowledge, his memories, his humor, his lusts, his passions, would be lost—synthesized into little fish parts. Tony felt a terrible sense of responsibility descend on him.

He got up and walked over to him. "Are you feeling better?"

Manny looked up. He was reading *Les Misérables*. "I am better. I haven't thanked you. You are a good leader and a brave companion. Without you I would have died."

"Forget it," Tony muttered.

"I do not forget such things. And, also, Christine behaved very well. She did not panic. She grabbed me but she did not lose the boat. She held on to both of us like a bulldog. It was no fault of hers that I was swept away. I am very impressed."

"Chris is a good sort. She's got a lot of backbone, really. I thought the bugs would be enough to send her packing, but she seems to be taking it all in stride." Smiling fondly, Tony looked over to her. She had fallen asleep over her notebook, her head nodding gently.

"But I worry, Manny. What will we do if there's an accident? We're weeks away from a hospital, and there's no way of communicating with the outside world. I've never been so cut-off before. In the service, there were support teams all over the place. It really makes you appreciate what all those explorers went through."

"We will take it a day at a time," Manny said. "We are a good expedition. Do not worry." He patted Tony's hand, then winked at him. "I have something that will cheer you up." He reached into his pack and pulled out another bottle of rum.

Tony whistled. "How many of those things have you brought?"

"A few. Liquor lightens the mood and makes the time pass happily." He leaned toward Tony, speaking in a low voice. "Sometimes, when I am just a little drunk, I begin to see things."

"What sort of things?" Tony asked suspiciously. "Pink elephants?"

"Women!"

"Go on, you're mad."

Manny uncorked the bottle. "Take a drink," he commanded. In obedience, Tony took a mouthful and swallowed it.

"Now, look at that tree," Manny said, pointing to one."

Tony stared. "All I see is a tree."

"It takes a few moments. See how it undulates, slowly, sensuously? Is it not as lissome as a dryad? Listen to the rustling. Is it not like the soft sounds of lacy underclothes being dropped by a bed? Of long, soft silk stockings brushing against each other?"

"Bloody hell," Tony whispered. He took another drink.

5

They woke at dawn to the unending chatterings, mutterings, and babblings of the jungle. Wherever they went, they were accompanied by this unseen chorus of animals. Only on occasion would the jungle reveal the abundance of life it supported. Then, springing into view like something from a magician's hat, a swirl of bats would appear, pollinating the brilliant flowers; or would see a small gray monkey curled in a tree, staring at them with dark, intense eyes.

They ate a breakfast of cold fish and rice—choking it down with cups of strong tea. The march to the Rio dos Mortes would be difficult. Tony showed them the route on the topo map, pointing out the many hills that separated them from their destination. Carrying the canoe would be burdensome, but unavoidable.

"Still," he said, "we should be able to do it in a day, so let's get going and get it over with."

Christine slipped on her pack, grunting at the weight. She was carrying a heavy load, as was Raeder. Tony and Manny were transporting the canoe, at least for the first leg. She and Raeder had split the supplies up between them.

"Everyone ready?" Tony asked. Each of them nodded, and they stepped off into the jungle.

The first hill, which was really just the river bank, was so steep it was easier to go up it on all fours holding on to saplings or tree trunks or creepers. After some unpleasant experiences, Christine quickly learned to inspect each handhold for thorns and ants.

The ridge at the top was narrow and they were suddenly on a steep downhill incline. Tony and Manny barely kept their footing. Christine and Raeder were thrown forward by the weight of their packs. Finally, they slid onto their chests and negotiated the steeper twists and turns by holding on to the lattice of roots that covered the ground.

By the third hill, they were all soaked with sweat and gasping for air. The heat was suffocating—an all-enclosing airlessness that radiated from the damp leaves and clammy ground. As they climbed, there were rare patches of sunlight where a tree had fallen.

The huge, rotten trunk would be sprouting fungi, heavy with moss and lichen, surrounded by dense, springing vegetation, and haloed by the unexpected light. But, otherwise, it was a world of endless twilight.

Tony was feeling giddy. The sweat towel he'd bound around his forehead was saturated. His shirt clung to him, as wet as if he'd thrown it in the river. He felt a rivulet of sweat drip down his chest, pool in his belly button, and trickle into his pants, washing away the zinc powder.

Behind him, he could hear Manny's rather labored breathing.

Trying to use the warm, scummy bathwater that had somehow gotten inside his skull and replaced his brain, he recalled some words of advice Major Essex had given him: "Try to think of nothing if the going gets tough. Or, if you're young enough (he had seemed dubious), think of sex. Never, ever think of the mountain that never gets any nearer."

So Tony thought of sex. He conjured up a vision of Christine, naked, sprawled on her bed. The image dissolved as the canoe dug unmercifully into his shoulder. Deciding that he would try for something a bit more abstract, he pictured a series of perky breasts, brown nipples, rounded buttocks, and long elegant thighs, but the sweat dripping into his eyes kept distracting him.

Desperately, he thought back to a woman who had been one of the first to set his hormones raging—Diana Rigg as Emma Peel, complete with black jumpsuit and champagne glass. Then the hill before him seemed to waver and fade into black. He dimly realized with real annoyance that he was, indeed, too old.

Surrendering, he held his arm up as a signal to halt. He examined everyone, noting that they all looked as though they were in the preliminary throes of cardiac arrest. Christine and Raeder had streaks of mud down their fronts. With their light-colored clothing, they looked like zebras.

"Anyone ready for a breather?" he asked,

trying to sound cheerful. No one answered, plainly because they were too tired to talk.

They threw themselves on the ground, waiting for their hearts to stop pounding. Finally, Christine said, "Is there any real need to treat this as an endurance test?" She glared at Tony. Continuing in an angry voice, she said, "Is it true we only need keep going down one hill and up the next until we get to the river?"

Tony nodded. "Good," she said. "In that case, *I'll* lead. That way, we can keep a sensible pace—which means a pace I can endure. I don't feel any obligation to prove *my* manhood. I think you're all as mad as hatters."

"What an admirable woman," Manny thought. "She has just saved us from death." Manny said aloud, shrugging, "Okay, it's all the same to me. How about it, Tony?"

"Oh, very well," Tony said. He tried to look as if he wouldn't mind taking the next stage as a sprint. Christine glowered at him and he smiled at her feebly.

Raeder, who was sitting next to Christine, wiped the sweat from his eyes, and then scrambled up with a yell. There was a leech on his arm. He pulled it off, but the leech looped over and sank its mouth into his palm.

Raeder began to dance, wriggling convulsively. He made a curious yelping sound. He pulled the leech off again, but this time it twisted around and began to drink at the base of his thumb.

"Shit," he screamed.

Manny pulled the leech out and smeared it on a tree. Christine shuddered and happened

to look at her legs. She looked again. They were
covered with undulating leeches. They were
edging up her trousers, looping up towards her
knees with alternate placements of their front
and rear suckers. With each rear attachment,
they waved their front ends in the air, seeming
to take a sniff. Plainly they smelled something
quite delectable. They were crawling on her
boots, too, and several particularly determined
individuals were trying to make their way in
via the airholes.

"Help," she screamed. She snatched at them
in handfuls and ground her bootheels into
them. "Get them off of me!" she cried.

"Look," Manny said, pointing to the ground.
There were more on the way, moving towards
them across the jungle floor from every angle, their
damp brown bodies half-camouflaged against the
rotting leaves. The place was infested. Leeches
were rearing up and sniffing from the trees, from
the leaves, and from the creepers.

"Oh God," Christine gasped, "but it looks
like the welcome wagon has arrived. They are
really pleased to see us."

They spent the next several minutes pulling
leeches off each other and wiping them on trees
or stomping on them. Hastily digging through
the packs, they brought out containers of zinc
powder and doused themselves, shaking the
stuff into their socks and trousers, filling their
boots and their underwear. With real trepida-
tion they sat down and waited.

Amazingly, the stuff worked. The leeches
looped toward them and then stopped midway

and midsniff, as though disgusted by something. They hesitated a bit, waving their heads in the air, undecided. Then clearly making up their minds that they were thoroughly revolted, they inched away. Something about their movements suggested they were off to file complaints with the management.

"Let's get out of here," Raeder said.

"Amen," Christine seconded.

"After you, then," Tony said, motioning her to the beginning of the line.

They set off at a more leisurely pace, a slow climb and descent which gave time to occasionally drink some water from the bottles at their belts and redust themselves with powder. Inspecting every tiny pool when they replenished the bottles, they noticed there was invariably a leech or two stretching out toward their hands. Christine thought about swallowing one and her stomach turned.

The day was as endless as the hills they climbed. Christine felt herself slipping into a sort of trance. All that mattered to her was continuing to put one foot in front of the other. She didn't believe they would ever actually arrive anywhere.

Laboriously they made their way gradually northwestward. Behind her, Christine heard Tony mumbling to himself. She strained to hear what he was saying. It sounded like:

> Fuck it!
> This sucks it!
> I'm stuck in
> This muck pit!

She was about to comment out loud on his poetic skills, similar in depth and passion to W. B. Yeats, when she realized what he was doing. "He's marching to it. It's a way of keeping up a steady beat."

She began to repeat the poem to herself, swinging her legs in rhythm to the lines. It seemed to help a bit. When things got a bit too dull, she tried to amuse herself by devising some variations. And so, softly chanting obscenities, they made their way to the Rio dos Mortes.

They reached the banks of the river just as the sun was setting. In a haze of exhaustion, they made camp. Tony insisted they eat, and he made a stew of rice and Spam, adding some chicken bouillon cubes for flavor. In the morning, they would begin their trip north on the Rio dos Mortes.

The next day the rain began. It fell in sheets, the monotony of its drumming on the canopy broken only by a series of thunderstorms. Manny warned them that the weather could last for days and that it was pointless to wait for it to clear. They launched the canoe.

As the days passed, the landscape altered even as they watched. Under the steady pounding, banks collapsed and trees tottered. Islands disappeared beneath the rising water. Formerly high knolls barely showed their muddy tops. The river became a latticework of waters—separate channels and tributaries splitting off, twisting back, interweaving and finally commingling again.

Swollen with rain, it was difficult to tell the difference between the river itself and side channels. With no familiar landmarks, Raeder and Manny investigated every current that moved north, trying to see if they were still on the river proper. Twice they moved completely in circles, and were only able to tell because of the ax marks and cleared ground of a camping spot.

Each evening they made camp in the rain and woke to the same sounds of rain pouring around them. Their hearing felt dulled and muffled. The world was an endless and unchanging gray, and they existed in it eternally wet, their senses shrouded. Fungus began growing on their clothes and hammocks. The sweet-sick smell of decay was ever present.

Mosquitoes were a constant torment. As long as the boat was in motion, few of them gathered, but when they stopped to make camp, the swarms were almost insupportable. They spent most of their time huddled in their hammocks, cowering inside the mosquito netting.

Raeder began having nightmares where he watched himself dissolve, fading into the curtain of rain until there was nothing left. He woke screaming night after night.

Christine lost track of the days. She had been keeping a journal, but each new entry was identical to the one before it. She began to lose interest, but Tony insisted she keep on with it.

"You'll become demoralized," he insisted.

"I think I already am." She was looking at her arms, which were covered with welts. She was horribly bitten and had been stung by wasps. "I look wretched and I feel wretched. I don't know if I've ever been this close to going stark-raving mad."

"Look," Tony said, "don't let your discipline drop. That'll be the end of it and we'll have to turn back. How'll you write that book if you don't have any notes?"

"But it seems so unnecessary. Nothing ever changes. The rain never stops and we eat the same things day after day—manioc and rice, smoked piranha, boiled piranha, piranha *au piquant* . . ." She got a wistful look on her face. "I think I'd kill for a pizza."

"I wouldn't mind a decent meal myself," he commiserated, patting her shoulder.

"I dream about food, Tony. I never used to be like this. I have incredibly sexual dreams involving butter and teacakes. Once I dreamt I was surrounded by pasta. Even when I'm awake, I find myself slipping off into fantasies about roast beef."

"Maybe we'll have some luck hunting." He pursed his lips. "Actually, I hope so. The rains are coming down fast and furious."

"So? What does that mean, except that we're even wetter than we were before?"

"It means the fish are going to be tough to get. They tend to hide at the bottom when it's raining hard."

Christine sighed. "I'm not sure if I care or not. There's always Spam and lentils." She tried to repress a shudder.

Tony looked at her. "Is it that bad, Chris?"

She smiled a little. "No, I suppose it's not. You know, sometimes I don't really believe in any of this. I'm convinced I must be dreaming. I think I'll wake up at home, in bed, ready for a day with Mother telling me I'm wasting my life.

"I feel like I should pinch myself sometimes to make sure I stay awake and alert. I don't know if my brain is willing to accept what a radical change I've made in my daily routine. It could barely cope when I gave up eating chocolate."

"You haven't given up eating chocolate," Tony said, puzzled.

"That's my point. I couldn't handle it. I had to renounce giving things up."

She continued, "Sometimes, I have visions of my brain curled up in a fetal position in a corner of my skull, screaming 'No, no.' And then it tries to convince itself that none of this is really happening, and it manufactures visions of clean clothes and cream buns." She paused. "Does that make any sense?"

"You're doing splendidly," Tony said, avoiding answering the question directly. "Manny thinks you're wonderful."

"He's rather wonderful himself." Christine chuckled. "Do you know how many women he's slept with? I wonder if he's telling the truth."

"I'm sure he is. I've known Manny long enough to realize he doesn't have any reason to make things up. His real life is fantastic enough. What do you think he dreams about?"

"Women, of course. This morning he told me he dreamt he was at a friend's house in Venezuela and two young girls were trying to pull down his trousers. Then a nun came along and chased them away. He's an incorrigible rip!''

She and Tony laughed for a bit and then he said, ''What do you think about Raeder?''

Christine shook her head slowly. ''I feel sorry for him. He's really going through a rough time. He seems competent enough, but I suspect this whole trip is nothing but a misery.''

''Do you think it's because this is a much longer trip than any he's taken?''

''Maybe that's part of it. But I think it's degrading for him to be wet and uncomfortable and doing physical work. I'll bet when he managed to escape from that Buenos Aires slum, he swore he'd never lift anything heavier than a telephone receiver again.''

''Could be. We'll have to try and keep him cheerful. Every once in a while he gets a blank, haunted look that scares the hell out of me. We're in a real jam if any of us breaks down.''

Three days later, the rains slackened and they emerged onto what was plainly the Rio dos Mortes. Dolphins played around the boat, and Manny spotted a swallow. Greatly cheered, Manny and Tony went hunting while Raeder and Christine made camp.

Eating manioc and piranha soup, Raeder asked question after question about London. He was extremely curious about the royal family and knew more about Charles and Di than Christine did.

''Someday I shall visit your lovely country,'' he said. ''I would very much like to see Buckingham Palace and the changing of the guard.

Also, Madame Tussaud's Wax Museum and the Tate.''

Christine laughed. ''You have quite a range of interests.''

''Yes, I am interested in everything. I would . . .''

Three shots interrupted him. He got up excitedly. ''Perhaps they have found something.''

Soon Manny and Tony appeared shouting wildly. They were dragging a dead tapir.

''I got the first shot,'' Manny yelled. ''Tony was quick, but I was quicker. He shot second.''

''We heard three shots,'' Christine said. ''Who was third?''

''What does it matter?'' Manny said, giving her a hug. ''We shall eat very well now.''

''It is well done,'' Raeder said, beaming. ''Tonight we'll cut it up and salt it down, and then we'll have enough meat to last us for months.''

Christine smiled broadly at the men, trying to match their enthusiasm. Inwardly, she felt a bit ill. The tapir was six feet long, compact and heavily built. Dull-green ticks were feeding all over its belly, neck, and genitals.

''Buck up, Chris,'' she told herself. ''At least it's not a piranha and, besides, there's not a McDonald's for a thousand miles.''

That evening they butchered the carcass, ate the liver, put their entire stock of salt over the strips and squares of meat, and sealed them in their biggest storage drum.

When they were done, Christine wiped her

bloody hands on her filthy pants. "Take that, Julia Child,"

They broke camp early, set off upriver and late in the afternoon rounding a bend into a straight stretch, were astonished to see a large plantation on the right bank. Two rectangular huts were set close by the shore, their windowless, thickly thatched roofs sloping right down to the ground on all sides. A haze of smoke diffused from the thatch into the sky.

A few large palms were still standing, but over several acres all the trees had been axed and burned, their great scorched trunks lying black and twisted among the new yucca plants and the young plantains.

There was a rustling noise down low at the end of the hut nearest to them and a thatched door, about three feet high, was thrown back. Two young women emerged, blinking in the sunlight. They stood and stared, slapping themselves as mosquitoes and blackflies bit their arms and legs.

Their glossy black hair was cropped short at the back of the neck and hung in a fringe across their foreheads. They were thickset and square-shouldered but no more than four and a half feet tall. Black lines drawn across their faces rippled as they smiled. Neither of them looked older than fifteen.

The smaller of the two had a matchstick stuck through a hole just below the center of her lower lip. Two other holes, deep and round, were at the corners of her mouth.

"Yanomani," Manny whispered.

"They look friendly enough," Christine whispered back.

"Wait until you see the men," he cautioned. "But this makes no sense, now that I think of it. They do not belong here. They are too far south; they do not grow manioc; and they are not really a river people."

A man came out of the hut. Circles and lines were drawn on his forehead and cheeks and he had long wooden plugs through the holes in his ears. He was holding a bow and two arrows.

"They look genuine enough for me. Do *you* want to tell him they don't belong here?" Tony asked Manny.

"I'd rather skip that for now."

Manny came slowly toward the man. "I speak their language a little. Let's see what we can find out." He called out to the man, who answered. A flurry of sound went between the two.

"His name's Jarivanu," Manny said, breaking off his conversation for a moment.

Whenever Manny's language skills failed, he helped himself with sign language and mime. He pointed to the women and made back and forth motions with his pelvis. Jarivanu grinned and nodded his head vigorously. The women broke into giggles.

"Those are his wives," Manny exulted. "We are understanding each other famously."

"Who says there isn't a universal language?" Christine said under her breath.

Jarivanu pointed toward Christine and asked

something. He was staring at her with real curiosity.

Manny turned toward her. He looked a little embarrassed. "How old are you, Christine? I am sorry, but he wants to know. It is best to be as accommodating as possible."

"I'm almost thirty. Why?" she asked in an irritated voice.

When Manny relayed this information, Jarivanu and his wives talked excitedly among themselves. Then Jarivanu motioned them to come into his hut.

"They are very honored to have you here," Manny said. He blushed. "They say you do not look old, but you are old inside." Christine winced.

"Old women have enormous status with the Yanomani. That is because they are so rare. Only an old woman can act as an ambassador and collect your dead warriors from the enemy. Also, they are the only ones who can carry messages between you and a hostile group. They are always treated better than anyone else in the tribe and have many privileges. I think everything will be duck soup for us from now on. Really, it is very lucky you came along, Christine!"

"Thanks ever so," she said, rather sharply. "Stand aside," she ordered, pushing Tony and Raeder out of the way. "Let Grandmother pass. Don't you have any respect for age?"

They unloaded the stores, setting aside bowls of manioc, spaghetti, and strips of tapir meat as presents to their host. Jarivanu helped them carry their cargo as they crouched low through the tiny door into the hut. Several small fires were burning on the mud floor and Manny hung up two kerosene lanterns, but it still took time for their eyes to adjust to the murk.

Several families lived inside, each with a segment of the hut to itself. A flimsy platform of long poles ran along the walls and held some baskets, a few pots, and some plastic bags. A narrow entrance at the back of the main hut led to a second, almost as large, in which many of the family spaces were empty. Jarivanu said that the main group was farther upriver. He and the others had come this far south to do some trading. Now they were on their way home.

Two old women squatted in a corner, hacking up yucca tubers with machetes. The younger mothers sat on the floor around the newcomers, unsmiling, and waiting, their babies on their laps or held firmly against their bodies with a cross-sling of red cloth. The men leaned against the support posts.

Raeder looked around the hut, an expression of despair on his face. "I cannot stand all this poverty. These people do not own anything. It is terrible . . . terrible."

"No fax machines out here," Tony said, grinning.

"No nothing out here. It is worse even than where I grew up. At least we had radios." Three dogs came up, sniffed his ankles, growled, and walked away.

"Buck up," Tony said, slapping him on the back.

Raeder gave him a look of utter contempt. "I will do my part to make sure these people do not murder us, but spare me your English hail-fellow-well-met cheeriness. It makes me sick."

He then announced loudly in Spanish that he was a cook to be reckoned with and would prepare a feast for everyone. Manny translated and the entire room looked at him with hopeful eyes.

"Of course, they are probably starving half the time," Raeder muttered under his breath, as he built a fire from a pile of split logs and wedged the cooking pots on top. "After this trip, I go to Rio and stay in a hotel. I find a girl who walks around wearing nothing but little Band-Aids on her private parts and we will make love and sit in the sand and get drunk."

Feeling a little awkward, Tony undid his canvas bag and took out his Polaroid, and also, a handful of brightly colored beads he had bought in London. Nervous, almost certain he was committing an act that reeked of nineteenth-century imperialism and cultural snobbery, he shared them out among the women. They took them eagerly, talking among themselves. Trading began immediately—the large, cheap red ones being worth about eight of the small, hand-painted, expensive variety.

Jarivanu squatted down and beckoned Manny to sit beside him. He patted the top of his own shaved skull and then ran his fingers through Manny's thick dark hair. With obvious amazement, he tugged at the mustache. Manny smiled benevolently and produced an enormous fart. Everyone laughed. The tension eased and the rest of the men sat down. Opening another bag, Manny produced fishhooks and line and shared them with the men.

They immediately began comparing their gifts, trying to measure and compare the length of each other's lines by stretching them diagonally from their big toe to their hand. The calculations, however, soon produced that look of irritation and anger which reminded Christine distinctly of her own involvement with mathematics. With a sudden shrug and a grin, they gave up.

Raeder announced the start of his banquet by banging the side of a cauldron with his ladle. "Ladies and gentlemen, dinner is served." He piled up one of the mess tins with hot rice covered in stewed tomatoes, cooked spaghetti, manioc, and pieces of tapir meat and handed it to the nearest Yanomani girl.

Jarivanu held up his hand, took the plate from the girl and handed it to one of the old women in the corner. Taking his cue, Raeder gave the next servings to the other old woman and Christine. Jarivanu nodded in approval. He gathered up each family's wooden bowls and supervised the rest of the meal's distribution.

The Yanomani licked their bowls clean and came back for second helpings. Tony realized how desperate a business finding enough food must be in such a place.

Jarivanu had chosen to eat with Manny and the two were engaged in slow, labored, but excited conversation.

"Christine," Manny bellowed. "I think we have hit the big time. Jarivanu has invited us back with him. We will see the entire group! And I think he knows something about your relatives."

"What?" Christine and Tony shouted. Jarivanu beamed at them in genial condescension.

"He says there are stories of some crazy white men coming to them. They were sick, one of them died. The others went to visit a haunted place and never came back."

"When was this?" Christine demanded.

"Long ago," Manny said. "They do not keep time the way we do. It was before the memory of anyone living. It is a story they tell."

Christine looked at Tony. She was excited. "Do you think there's anything in it?"

"It's certainly worth investigating. And it would be interesting to see how these people live. It's why we're here, after all."

"What is this haunted place he mentions?" Christine asked Manny.

After more conversation, Manny said, "It is a sacred place on a high hill. Spirits live there and it is very dangerous. Mortals who trespass are punished. Either they never return or they are found mad. No one goes there anymore."

"Tell him nothing could keep us away," Christine said urgently. "You don't think he'll change his mind, do you?"

"Certainly not," Manny said, offended. "He is an honorable and respected man."

"Let's take a picture," Tony said enthusiastically. "This moment should be memorialized." He picked up the Polaroid, fitted in a bar of flash bulbs and, in the ensuing silence, took Jarivanu's photo. The dogs yelped at the burst

of light and crept behind a pile of logs. Everyone tensed. The men stood up.

Manny paled. ''My God, Tony, what have
you done?''

Swallowing, Tony gave the still-wet print to
Jarivanu. Gradually, the image appeared. The
Yanomani jostled around warily and then, as
the face became unmistakable, they grinned
with delight. Barely able to conceal his relief,
Tony took pictures of everyone. Raeder looked
as if he was going to faint.

Manny, recovering himself, suddenly realized that he was alive, that he had not been
bashed by a club or shot with arrows, that
he was relatively dry, that he was free of mosquitoes, that he was surrounded by friendly,
half-naked girls, and that life was good. In a
pleasant baritone he began to sing. He performed Mexican love songs, arias from Mozart
operas, the latest Venezuelan pop songs, and
''Rule, Britannia.'' Eventually, exhausted, he
turned to his audience and indicated that now
they should sing their songs.

The girl with the matchstick marshalled all
the young mothers into a line and began a high-
pitched, nasal, dissonant chant to which the
others provided a chorus. They stood quite still
as they sang their eerie song, impassive, unsmiling, without moving their hands or feet,
and after about five minutes, they all sat down.
The expedition members clapped and shouted
for more, but Jarivanu, shaking his head, got
up, went to his hammock, and came back carrying a long reed pipe, about two and a half

feet long, with a nozzle at one end, and a small
phial of brown powder.

"*Yappo*," he said.

Manny groaned. "What is it?" Tony whispered to him.

"It is a drug—a hallucinogen. It is given to
the leader of another group as a gesture of
friendship. To refuse it would be a grave insult.
It would be a declaration of intent to make
war."

"Oh, Tony," Christine whispered.

"I will take it," Manny said. "You do not
need to do this, Tony."

"Nonsense," Tony said stoutly. "I'm the
leader and I'll do as I should. How bad can it
be? They're all healthy."

Jarivanu tipped a small amount of powder
into his thick palm and carefully tipped it into
the open end of the pipe. Then he offered it to
Tony, motioning him to put the nozzle into a
nostril.

Tony hesitated briefly, and then followed Jarivanu's instructions. He shut his eyes. Jarivanu
took in an enormous breath of air and blew long
and hard down the tube.

To Tony, it seemed as if someone had just hit
him over the bridge of his nose with a small
log. He grabbed the back of his head to keep it
from detaching itself and rolling around on the
ground. Someone shoved a burning stick down
his throat. His lungs filled with hot ash. There
was no water anywhere. Dimly, he realized Jarivanu was offering him the reloaded pipe.

His ears, nose, and throat went into shock.
He sat, unable to breathe, his head between his

knees. And then, suddenly, he was gulping oxygen through a clogging goo of snot. Every mucous membrane he possessed was vomiting out its contents.

The pain left. He realized that it was all over, that he was still alive and breathing better than he ever had in his life. He looked up. Two of the Yanomani men were squatting on either side of him, their arms around his shoulder. He saw that Jarivanu had just received a dose of *yappo* and was being sick by a support pole. Tony smiled graciously.

It was eminently clear to him that the Yanomani were the kindest, most benevolent people on earth. He felt physically invulnerable: A mere bash on the head from a club would be a minor inconvenience, at most. The hut had grown enormously. There was plenty of room for everyone. Glancing around, he noticed how homelike everything seemed, how touchingly familiar. It occurred to him that becoming a Yanomani would be a desirable and simple thing to do. He could sit here forever.

He looked around, his eyes radiating goodwill toward all. He noticed Christine sitting only a few feet from him. "Are you all right, Tony?" she asked anxiously. "You've got the silliest expression on your face."

"I'm wonderful," he sighed. He smiled back at her, giddy with tenderness and desire. She appeared to him perfect in every way. He could make love to her forever, which is exactly how much time he had. It stretched before him in all directions, as wide as the jungle.

He admired her, savoring each particle of her

beauty. In his imagination, he stroked her neck, running his hands through the tangled brown hair. He kissed her nose, her calloused hands. He ran his fingers over her shoulders and back. For several years, he ran his tongue over her thighs, savoring each cut, each bruise, each insect bite.

Suddenly, powerful hands grabbed him from behind. He tried to shake himself free but couldn't. He stared up into Manny's face.

"Get up," Manny said. "It is time for sleep."

Tony protested incoherently, but Manny was firm. "Do you know you have been staring at Christine for several hours?"

"I was only looking," Tony said grumpily. "And what's wrong with that? She's my woman, after all."

"In Yanomani eyes she is an old woman. She should be venerated, but not looked at with such lust. I'm afraid you've shocked them terribly. They have great doubts about your morals."

"Quite revolting behavior," Raeder said. "You must learn to control yourself."

"I didn't do anything," Tony sulked. "Where's Chris?"

"With the other women," Manny said. "She'll sleep with them." He chuckled. "They think she needs protecting."

6

The next morning, they prepared for their journey upriver to the Yanomani homeland. Tony noticed that the men occasionally looked over at him and laughed. Once in a while a warrior, for no apparent reason, would come over and clap him on the shoulder. Christine, on the other hand, was barely civil.

"What's going on?" he asked Manny.

"I think you embarrassed Christine last night," he answered. "I've never seen such a look of exalted lechery on a man's face. So she is not too pleased with you. On the other hand, the Yanomani men believe you can screw everything that moves. A woman her age is getting quite beyond that sort of thing in their culture. I think they are a little envious and a little impressed."

Tony was absurdly pleased. The Yanomani's reaction made him feel like a member of the group and an exceptionally virile one to boot. He swaggered over to Christine. "Good morning, love."

She glared at him. "You should be ashamed of yourself. I've never seen anyone behave so disgracefully at a party before. I know this isn't

Mayfair, but that's hardly any reason to throw all decorum to the winds."

"It was the drug, Chris. Give me a break. I didn't know what I was doing."

She snorted. "Drugs lower inhibitions—they don't give you brain transplants. I thought it was bad enough when you got drunk at my friend Nan's party and went around telling everyone you were really the Falcon and could leap tall buildings at a single bound, and then jumped off the the coffee table into the philodendrons . . ."

"I recovered very nicely from that jump. It's because I know how to fall."

"You may have recovered, but the philodendrons didn't. I don't think Nan did, either. Every time I mention your name, I can see she barely suppresses the urge to gather her flora to her bosom like an overprotective nature goddess. It's very irritating. She always gets this incredibly superior look on her face. Then she manages to mention how her Clive has gotten another raise or promotion or some other tangible evidence of his superiority over the rest of mankind. Why anyone would want to marry a damn Boy Scout is beyond me."

"She's a stuck-up snob. I don't know why you see her."

"That's not the point. I see many people I think are unpleasant. It always makes me feel very enlightened and superior. The point is that I don't relish this expedition becoming wellknown among the populace because it's led by a sex maniac."

"I don't see why you should mind. Apparently the Yanomani already know your family is crazy. Percy managed to establish that quite nicely."

Christine gritted her teeth. "I think we'll leave personal comments about the sanity of our relatives out of this. Aren't you the one with the uncle who goes out after rainstorms to poke the worms with his cane and scream, 'You haven't got me yet, you bastards?'

"Also, perhaps I should mention that our hostesses had quite a few questions about you, which they asked after you went to bed. We had a very pleasant little hen party."

"You're bluffing. You can't speak their language."

"I took a lesson from Manny's book. You'd be amazed what you can accomplish with pantomime."

Tony looked a little nervous. "What exactly did you tell them?"

"Just the truth, darling. Just the bare truth." She kissed him on the nose and walked away.

Tony looked over at the matchstick girl who was loading cargo into the canoe. She caught his glance and burst out in laughter.

"When I get back, I'm retiring," he muttered. "I'm going to become something peaceful and relaxing—like a war correspondent." It began to rain again.

After three days of traveling, they came to a landing stage. Tony turned to Jarivanu, who was riding in their canoe, and with his fingers, mimed someone walking. Then he pointed in the direction of the jungle.

Jarivanu smiled comfortably and pointed, too. Then he said something, waving his hand about in an offhand way. Clearly, he didn't take whatever was coming next very seriously.

Manny said, "I think he's telling us how far we have to walk. I think he says it's not far, but God knows what that means—we'll never be able to go at his pace."

Raeder pulled nervously at his lower lip. "If we walk into this land, anything could happen. We aren't welcome here. I think we should turn back."

"I appreciate your fears," Tony said. "I've got to go on. But I don't want to put pressure on anyone else." He looked around. "What Raeder said is correct—it is dangerous. Anyone who wants to come with me is welcome, but there's no shame for anyone who wants to stay behind." He paused. "What about you, Chris?"

"It's why I've come. If there's a chance they know something about Grandfather, I certainly can't go back."

Manny tugged at his mustache. "I will go. I will write a monograph on the Yanomani and submit it to the Royal Geographic Society. They will be sure to accept it. Perhaps I will get a knighthood." Christine and Tony looked at him in utter disbelief. "You never know," he said, shrugging his shoulders.

Shamed, Raeder said, "Very well, I will not be the only one to hang back. But you will please note my objections."

"Of course," Tony said. "I appreciate your honesty."

Manny drew Tony aside. "We must be careful of him. He is afraid and does not wish to come."

"We're all afraid, or should be," Tony said. "I'll try to keep an eye on Raeder."

"There is something else that worries me."

"What's that?"

Manny jerked his head in Jarivanu's direction. "Him."

"I really don't think he means to hurt us. We made a good impression on him the other night and I think Christine, considering her exalted status, is going to be like a talisman for us."

"Don't be a fool," Manny said impatiently. "That is not what I mean. I am worried that we are not strong enough. We will have to keep up with him for hours at least—maybe days. Who knows what he means by 'not far'? What I consider a major trek is nothing but a little jog for him."

"Maybe it won't be so bad," Tony said stoutly. He decided not to mention that he had been secretly hoping Jarivanu might only have one lung, or be arthritic, or a devoted bird watcher. "And if it gets to be too much for us, he'll just have to stop. After all," he said in a low voice, "we have an old woman with us."

Manny's eyes lit up. "Of course. You think of everything, Tony."

Jarivanu and the other Yanomani had gone off into the forest. They returned with long bundles of green palm fronds and began to plait the leaves together. In a few minutes they had packs, each one capable of holding sixty pounds. Using bark, they made headbands and shoulder straps. Jarivanu kept one and passed out the others to the expedition members. The other Yanomani would come no farther.

All the remaining plastic bags of beads, fishhooks, fishing line, mirrors and combs, medicines, machetes, and half the remaining food—salt, sugar, coffee, corn flour, and lentils, were parceled out.

They formed up behind Jarivanu. He had his head forced down to his shoulders by the weight of the pack pulling on the strap across his forehead. His face looked red with pressure and excitement. Tony had given him a new machete as a gift and he held it tightly in one hand. He was grinning broadly. In Tony's mind he had a horrible resemblance to a racehorse in top condition, straining at the bit, eager for the race.

Responding suddenly to some psychic starter's gun, he bounded off into the jungle. A groan rose from the members of the expedition and they set off after him.

Four foot six inches tall, brutally fit, Jarivanu slipped under vines that caught the others around the waist. He stooped under the branches of fallen tree trunks that forced his companions to take off their packs and crawl on all fours. His bare feet propelled him through the small creeks and up their soft, dark, rotted banks without a change in his half-loping rhythm.

But what impressed Tony most was that he was constantly alert. Despite the weight hanging from his head which made the tendons of his neck stand out like sticks, he kept scanning the underside of the canopy for fruit, for bees' nests, for the movement of leaves that might betray a monkey.

"I'd give my right arm to have a unit made up of these fellows," he thought, through a haze of fatigue.

As the afternoon sweated on, Jarivanu seemed less eager to push ahead. He was plainly looking for something. The ground became firmer, the trees bigger. And then finally, he halted.

Since this respite was plainly the result of a miracle, everyone gathered around him, trying to see if he had been hit by lightning or was simply overcome with remorse for his brutal treatment of his friends. It was neither. They had come to a path. There was no doubt about it. It was well-used and four feet wide.

Tony turned to his exhausted troops. "Follow the yellow brick road," he said, pointing to the path.

Raeder looked at it glumly. "Now we can all die together," he said. "Just to please Tony. Just to see what it's like."

The path led to a plantation. The ground had been completely cleared and sunlight poured down on them. They blinked stupidly.

"It's been so long," Christine said. She stretched her arms out to it, as if she would embrace the light to her body.

Raeder said, "Tony, take our picture." He rummaged through his pack and brought out the Polaroid. His movements were exaggeratedly calm, and Tony realized it was to keep his hands from shaking.

It was, Tony thought, a bizarre request. But he thought he knew what Raeder was thinking. Perhaps, someday, a missionary or anthropologist would come to this place and find a rusty, unopened camera—and the small mystery of the disappearance of the second Fawcett expedition would be explained.

Tony smiled, motioned Manny, Raeder, and Christine into a group and said, "Say cheese." He snapped the photo. Then he turned and looked straight at the shafts of two six-foot-long arrows, fitted, he noticed with preternatural clarity, with notched, needle-sharp, curare-dipped tips. The two young men holding the fully drawn bows stood with arched backs and expressionless faces.

"Hullo," he said stupidly.

Jarivanu grabbed Tony's hat from his head and waved it around, shouting. The young men lowered the bows and smiled. More people began running toward them. Tony breathed. Jarivanu pointed to Christine and said something else. The Yanomani gave a long "Aaaaah."

An old woman elbowed everyone aside and stood in front of her. She had spindly legs, a slack belly, and enormous hanging triangles of breasts. Her eyes looked kind and grandmotherly. Gently, she patted Christine on the cheeks, smiling and nodding at her.

Christine's heart melted. The woman said something to her in a low, soft voice, and she was certain it was along the lines of "My goodness, you've grown so! But you're so thin.

Don't worry, darling, I've made all your favorites. We'll put some meat on your bones.'' It was no surprise when the woman dragged her over to a cooking fire and gave her a wooden bowl filled with cooked plantains.

That evening there was a feast. Christine, seated in a place of honor with the other old women, clapped and shouted as Jarivanu performed a fearsome dance to the beat of a skin drum.

He crouched in the center of the room. With exaggerated movements, his thigh muscles bunching and loosening, intense concentration on his face, he turned slowly in time with the music, first on one foot and then on the other, rising, inch by inch to his full height, apparently peering over some imaginary cover.

Sighting the enemy, he crouched again, and then, as the music quickened, he drew his club and leaped violently forward, weaving and dodging with immense exertion, cutting and striking, parrying unseen blows. For a small second, his ghostly foe was off-guard, tripped, and Jarivanu claimed his victory with one malicious blow.

Tony was enthralled. One of the warriors had given him another dose of *yappo* and he had again achieved that state of hyperawareness and well-being that characterized the drug. The world was a beautiful place and so were its people.

He realized that Jarivanu was dragging him onto center stage. The room rang with cheers and claps. They wanted him to perform. He smiled. It would, he thought, be simplest to copy Jarivanu's basic steps. There was not much to it, after all. The music began again, sounding just a little bit stranger to him than it had before.

Tony began the slow crouch on one leg, turning slightly. "Perhaps," he thought, "this is not the best way to begin." Ghastly pains ran up his thighs. He noticed, with irritation, that some silly girl was tittering. The silly girl was Christine. He glared at her. She clapped a hand over her mouth.

Cramps hit both buttocks at once and his back began to wobble. His arms waved wildly and he sat down hard on the ground. There was an uproar in the hut.

Looking as dignified as he could, Tony stood up. He peered over an imaginary boulder and looked straight into the eyes of a very real old man. "What's that old fool laughing at?" he thought.

Waving his imaginary club, he advanced upon the foe. He felt lithe and dangerous—a jaguar hunting his prey. The old man fell off his seat. There was so much hilarity, so much sidesplitting laughter, Tony couldn't hear the drum, and so thought that perhaps his rhythm might not be all that it should.

"Tony," Manny shouted, gasping for breath, "don't let him get away!" He was pounding Jarivanu on the back.

Stung to the quick by this mockery from one who owed him his very life, Tony advanced upon Manny, grabbed his arm and yanked him upright. "Let's see you do better," he said. He thrust the imaginary club into Manny's hand.

With great presence, Manny advanced to the stage. The room fell silent. A veteran of a thousand confrontations with hostile natives, hostile governments, and aggrieved husbands, he regarded his audience with calm authority. His huge brown eyes appeared to fix on everyone in turn. There was some backward shuffling in the front row. A dog whimpered.

The music began a little shakily. Manny, in time to the music, began to mime. He was hunting something. He made rooting motions with his head and grunting sounds. It was immediately apparent he was hunting a wild pig. He leaped and smashed downward with the club. He howled in triumph. The room exploded in applause.

But he wasn't done. He butchered the pig, selected the joint he wanted to eat, and hung the carcass from a hook in the roof. Holding the joint aloft, he marched triumphantly into his ideal kitchen.

Passion entered his performance and the drummer increased his tempo out of sympathy. He scored the pork, he stuffed it. The room became redolent with the smell of herbs. Basil and sweet rosemary scented the air. Sharp, crisp apples were diced, mixed with onions, and stuffed inside the pork.

The meat was rubbed with garlic, caressed with seasonings. It was roasted and basted. It turned brown and succulent. Broccoli, asparagus, and artichokes were steamed; elaborate sauces were concocted.

And then Manny ate. No one had ever eaten the way Manny ate that night. He savored the meat, he relished the crackling, he sucked the bones with gusto. The gravy was perfect, the applesauce was sweet. A bottle of burgundy sat by his side and he toasted his own efforts. At the meal's completion, he burped. The room rose to its feet.

"Bravo," Tony shouted. "Bravissimo."

The formal gathering broke up into small groups, drinking, laughing, and telling stories. The largest circle was around Manny, who was plainly the social success of the evening. Tony was feeling a bit wobbly in the legs and Christine rushed over to support him.

"Ask Jarivanu to tell the story about my family," she said to Manny. Manny translated, pointing to Christine. He listened carefully to Jarivanu's lengthy reply.

"It is as he told us before. Long years ago, three white men came here. One of them died. He had been very sick. The two others went to the home of the spirits who live on the far hill. Of course, they never returned. That is all he knows. He says they were insane, that all the people warned them not to go. He wants to know if you are crazy, too."

"What does he think?" Christine asked with some asperity.

"He thinks yes."

"I'm so glad I asked," Christine muttered. "Can he show us where to find this spirit dwelling?"

Again, Manny listened to Jarivanu who

seemed upset, and waved his arms to emphasize his words.

"If we insist, he can guide us part of the way. He will not go there himself. He begs you not to go. He says you will certainly die, which would mean great sadness for him. He wants us to stay here. The more old women the better, and that Tony makes them laugh harder than anyone they have ever met." He beamed. "He says that I will make a great warrior."

Tony snorted. "You simply seduced them with your superior cooking skills. How was I to know we'd stumble on a lost tribe of incipient gourmets?"

"Really, we must go on," Christine insisted. "These people are lovely, but we do have the expedition to consider. Besides, I'm getting tired of being reminded of my age. They're all beginning to sound like Mother. I just know one of them is gearing up for a lecture on why I should get married and settle down. I haven't traveled thousands of miles just to hear that all over again."

"Hear, hear," Tony said.

"I would rather go than stay," Raeder said, coming up to them. "Any place they are afraid to go sounds like a good place to me."

"Now, now," Tony said, clapping him on the back, "they've been very nice to us."

"Yes, but who knows how long it will last. Once we have given away all the mirrors and beads and fishhooks, perhaps they will tire of us."

"They seem to like us for ourselves," Tony

said, rather hurt. "I don't think you should ascribe mercenary instincts to them."

"They won't laugh at your jokes forever," Raeder answered.

"I don't know," Tony said. "I was thinking of staging a performance of *Hamlet*. I think it would go over rather well. It has all the right ingredients. We'd have to pantomine the whole thing but that's fine—we don't know the lines anyway."

Christine giggled.

"I do not think it is funny," Raeder said rather huffily. He stalked off.

"Poor man," Christine said. She yawned. "I'm exhausted. Thank Jarivanu for the lovely evening. I don't know when I've enjoyed myself more. His parties are much better than Nan's, and the people are so much more agreeable." With a weary wave, she stumbled off to bed.

Jarivanu said something to Manny. "What's he saying?" Tony asked.

"He wants to know if she is really mad. He wants to know if all white people are mad."

"Tell him yes. Bloody loonies, each and every one of us."

Manny translated and Jarivanu answered. "He says he thought so."

Tony also went off to bed, exhausted from the longest day he ever hoped he'd have. Occasionally, sounds pierced the fog of sleep. The last thing he remembered was Manny singing "Waltzing Matilda," and teaching the chorus to the Yanomani.

* * *

The next morning, after a leisurely breakfast, they again got ready to leave. Jarivanu agreed to take them close enough to the site of the spirits' home so they could find the rest of the way themselves.

He was disconsolate, certain he was sending these amusing and foolish people to their deaths. In his brief acquaintance with them it had become eminently clear that they had no idea what they were doing and were, mentally, little more than babies. The one called Manny showed some promise as a storyteller, but the others were hopeless. Clearly, letting them wander about on their own was signing their death warrant.

When the women heard of Christine's plans they broke into a resounding wail. She shivered. Their noise sounded too much like a dirge to suit her.

"What do you think the spirits' house is like?" Christine asked Tony nervously. "My bet is for some sort of ghastly suburban villa. No wonder these people won't go near it." She tried to laugh.

"I've no idea what this is about," Tony said. "If Jarivanu says there's something there to be afraid of, I'm willing to take him at his word. He hardly strikes me as a coward."

"Of course he's not. But who knows what things do scare him. Manny says they have all sorts of complex beliefs about wandering souls and sympathetic magic. He says it's a big mistake to look at them living in the forest and think of them as free spirits. He says that's nonsense and romanticism. They're as bound

up in propitiations and rules of etiquette and
protocol as anyone we've ever met."

"Maybe there's nothing haunted about this
place at all," she continued hopefully. "Maybe
there's nothing there. It could be symbolic,"
she finished, rather lamely.

"Look," Tony said, "I hope there's no big,
bad wolf waiting for us out there just as much
as you do. There's simply no point in speculat-
ing, though. We'll know soon enough."

"I suppose." Christine sighed.

Manny and Raeder came over. "Are you
ready? Jarivanu is anxious to get started. He
will not stay in the area after dark."

"Ready as I'll ever be," Christine said. "I'll
bet it's snakes," she said under her breath.

They began another grueling march. Jarivanu
was plainly in a hurry. "Why doesn't this ever
get any easier?" Christine thought, staggering
under her load. A branch hit her in the face.
"There's got to be a better way to travel."

Several hours later they came to their first
deep river, about thirty yards across. After
carefully inspecting its bark and crown, Jarivanu selected a tree which, to Christine's eye,
looked exactly like all the rest. She slipped off
her pack and, as her legs gave way, sat down
on it. There would be at least a half hour's wait
while Jarivanu fashioned a bridge. She would
have time to leisurely drink a whole bottle of
water. She stretched out and sighed.

Jarivanu hit the tree at chest height with a
flurry of machete blows, grinning all the while.
He stood for a minute in a shell burst of white

wood fragments. The tree creaked forward, let down slowly by a tangle of vines, and toppled across the river. It was obviously the softest tree in the forest. There would be no rest for anyone.

Christine struggled to her feet. She smiled brilliantly at Jarivanu. "It may not be fair," she thought, "and it may not be just, but right now, I hate that man."

Jarivanu set off happily along his bridge, his feet gripping the trunk as if they had suction pads on their soles. He lopped off branches and vines as he went, clearing a passage.

Tony called a halt. "Just a minute, please." He cut a sapling for everyone. "Use these to keep your balance, and no one crosses with a pack on their back. If you fall in, it'll hold you down." He waved Jarivanu back and gave him his pack. Jarivanu trotted with it to the other side.

Using the pole like a tightrope walker, he crossed to the far bank. "Christine," he shouted, "give your pack to Jarivanu, and then come over."

"It doesn't look so hard," she thought, setting across. Her boots seemed to give no purchase on the slimy bark. The pole took on a life of its own, wobbling to left and right. The river tilted up to look at her on one side, lay flat, and then repeated the process with an increase in tempo. She fell. The world went black and gurgled.

Then there was a push on her chest. She choked, spluttered, and gulped air. Through the water streaming down from her hat, still

held in place by the chin strap, she looked into
Manny's slightly hooded, dark brown eyes. He
was treading water, roaring with laughter.

When she emerged on the far bank, Jarivanu
and Tony were laughing, too. "What," she said
with as much dignity as she could muster, "is
so funny? I almost drowned."

"Sorry, Chris," Tony said, wiping his eyes.
"I wouldn't have laughed if you'd drowned."

"Well, thank you very much. I find that an
extremely comforting sentiment." She stood
there dripping and staring at Tony with accus-
ing eyes.

"You look like one of those ghastly women
in Victorian ghost stories who wander around
in dank winding-sheets, with their heads
tucked underneath their arms," he said, grinning.

She sneezed at him.

But Raeder, when he came across, was anxious, and stern. "What will we do? What will
we do if another group kills Jarivanu? What
will we do if we have to run from the Yanomani?" No one could answer him.

For the next three rivers, Christine simply
gave her pack to Jarivanu and swam across. The
soakings made little difference at this point. She
was as wet as she could possibly get.

Finally, Jarivanu halted and stood still, waiting for them to catch up. When they stood there
in a group, gasping, sweat running down their
bodies, he herded them to the top of a hill. At
the crest, he pointed.

Christine craned her neck. All she could see were trees. "What is it?" she asked.

Manny, who was the tallest, stared down. "My God, there's some sort of stone building out there in that valley. I can see little bits of the top. It's hard to get a clear view, there are so many trees." He sat down hard on the ground. "This is not possible. There should be no buildings here whatsoever. It is unknown."

"I think I see," Raeder said. "I see stone, too. Ask what this means," he said to Manny.

But Jarivanu was already speaking. His words came quickly, urgently. He waved his arms to emphasize what he was saying.

"I can't get it all," Manny said. "But, assuming the white men who visited the Yanomani were Percy and Jack Fawcett, this is where they came. This is where they disappeared. Jarivanu wants us to come back with him and he absolutely refuses to go any farther. He says the place is haunted." Manny sighed. "He's probably right."

"We've got to go on," Christine said. "We've already settled it. I'll be damned if I turn back without getting a good look at that building."

Manny turned to Jarivanu and explained. "Try to tell him," Christine said "how very much we appreciate all he's done for us. I don't know how we could have survived."

"I think he knows that," Manny said.

"Yes, I suppose there is no point in belaboring the obvious." She thought a moment and then unfastened a gold chain she always wore around her neck. It had been a present from

Tony. "Sweetheart, I want to give him this. Is it all right?"

"Of course it's all right," Tony said. "It's little enough for what he's done. If it would do him any good, I think I'd give him all my stock in IBM."

Christine handed the chain to Jarivanu. His face lit up. Gently, he patted her cheek. She thought she was going to burst into tears.

Jarivanu walked down the hill away from them. At the base, he looked up and waved. Then, with no warning, he was gone. He had vanished into the rain forest as if he were a ghost.

Utter desolation settled on them. With the Yanomani, the jungle had become a human place where people could live and be at home. Now it again appeared alien and unknowable. They felt lost, abandoned, adrift in a dangerous world. Which is exactly what they were.

"Well," Christine said, wiping her eyes, "I'm sure we'll see him again on the way back. We'll only be gone a few days."

"That's right," Tony said, hugging her. "I'm quite certain of the way back, but even if I thought I couldn't find him again, I'm sure he'll find us."

"Let's get this over with," Raeder said. "If there are any spirits in this place, I would prefer meeting them by daylight."

They trudged down the hill in silence. A dark cloud had fallen on them.

Settling into their own pace, they moved slowly, climbing one hill, descending, and find-

ing another facing them. On the downhill
slopes, the tip of the building disappeared, but
became visible again on the ascents. They at
least were in no danger of losing their way.

Tony kept referring to his topo maps, trying
to keep track of where they were but it was
hopeless. The area was almost totally uncharted. It was like looking at a map from the
age of exploration, where unknown areas were
marked with sea monsters and a legend that
said "Here be dragons." Although his own
chart was much more scientific looking and
scorned all such fanciful decoration, for all
practical purposes the result was the same. He
took frequent sightings of the building, mark-
ing down the compass readings. He felt confi-
dent that between his own efforts and the
bridges they'd chopped down, he could guide
them back safely to the Yanomani settlement.

At last they came to a ring of hills so steep
they were more like small mountains. The for-
bidding cliffs looked like a fortress. "Does anyone else get the feeling we've come to a sort of
natural wall?" Christine asked.

Manny nodded. "I agree. I believe our quest
lies on the other side of these. Somebody was
very concerned that the building would be well
hidden."

"And easy to defend," Tony added.

They began to climb, scrambling for hand-
holds among the roots and vines, pausing to
gasp for breath, and then moving again. They
kept glancing anxiously at the sky, noting how
low the sun was getting. It was late afternoon,

and they hadn't eaten since breakfast, and they still hadn't reached the top.

"I certainly hope there's no vampires out here," Christine said, between labored breaths.

"There are vampire bats in this area," Manny said helpfully.

"Manny," Christine said in a voice of exaggerated patience, "when I want the truth I'll ask for it."

At last they reached the top and looked straight into the valley below. For a moment, they were speechless.

7

It was a pyramid, a succession of progressively smaller rectangles laid one atop the other, and it rose up a hundred feet from the valley floor. A stairway, like a gigantic ramp, slanted up one side. "It looks Mayan," Manny said. His voice cracked. "That makes no sense. The Mayans never came this far south."

He looked desperately at Christine. "Do you see the same thing I do, or am I having a hallucination? I see a big pyramid with steps."

"I see it," she said soberly. "But I don't believe it."

"A McDonald's would be more plausible," Manny said, with wonder in his voice.

"Let's get down there," Tony said.

They scrambled down the hill, tripping over their own feet. The pyramid loomed below them and showed no sign of dissolving like a mirage in the desert. It looked quite convincingly real.

When they reached it, they touched the blocks of stone hesitantly, as though they expected the structure to burst like a soap bubble. "Percy's lost city," Christine said. "He finally found it. Can you imagine how ecstatic he must have been?"

"It is the find of the century," Raeder said, almost to himself. "I wonder what is inside." He pointed to a chamber set at the top of the stairway. An entrance was clearly visible.

"Look," Tony said, "this is all incredibly exciting but it's almost sundown. We need to make camp. I don't want anyone going into this place tonight. We'll wait for daylight. There's too many stories of people going mad or simply disappearing, for me to want to rush in. We'll start exploring tomorrow."

Manny nodded. "Yes, old stones do not eat men. Something else around here is hungry." He looked at Tony. "What do you think about posting a guard tonight?"

"I'm for it. Why don't we split it—I'll take one half and you the other."

"Good. I'd like the first half if you don't mind. I enjoy the jungle nights. So," he said, rubbing his hands together, "let's get started."

That evening, over dinner, Christine asked, "Who do you think could have built this place?"

"It beats me," Tony said. "What do you say, Manny? It looked familiar to you."

"To me, as I said, it looks Mayan. This is, of course, unheard of. The Mayans are in Mexico, Guatemala, northern Honduras, and El Salvador. There are many mysteries about them, though. I suppose it is possible that some could have come this far into South America. This discovery will make us very famous. I think it will rival the finding of Tutankhamen's tomb.''

He leaned back, picking his teeth, grinning happily. ''You see, Raeder. You come with us and your fortunes improve. Because of this expedition you will be able to go home and set up another agency for the rich tourists. You will have two fax machines and a beautiful, voluptuous secretary. Will she be dark or fair, I wonder.''

''What do you think is inside?'' Raeder said, ignoring Manny's speculations. ''Perhaps there are valuables within which are worth much money.''

''I'm sure the Brazilian government will have something to say about it if there are,'' Tony broke in. ''I want to be very clear about this. If we attempt to smuggle out anything we find, then we're subject to prosecution. I strongly suspect Brazilian jails to be unpleasant in the extreme.''

''It does not seem fair,'' Raeder said. ''We take the risks and do all the work. Are we to get nothing for it?''

''We'll get recognition and there'll be all sorts of publicity. But as for taking things that legally belong to someone else, that's out. I hope I make myself clear.''

''Of course,'' Raeder said, shrugging. ''It is your expedition, after all. You make the rules.''

''I didn't make these rules—the government did.''

''Of course, of course,'' Raeder said. ''I understand.'' He looked at Tony hopefully. ''Perhaps we will get on talk shows?''

"Could be," Tony said, not sure if he was exasperated or amused.

"I would like that," Raeder said. "I very much want to recover my fortunes. Perhaps this is indeed the way to doing it."

Manny and Tony exchanged glances. Christine looked uneasy. "There probably isn't anything here," she said. "If nothing else, the place has probably been looted a hundred times. We know we're not the only people who know about it. After all, the Yanomani showed it to Grandfather."

"That's so," Tony said. "I wouldn't doubt that some of the people who disappeared took a powder after selling some artifacts to some trader or another."

"Of course, that wouldn't account for Grandfather. If he came here, he would have told the world. This would have bolstered all his cockeyed theories about lost worlds and Atlantis."

"We know he came here," Tony said, "but we don't know this is the last place he was. All we know is that he didn't return to Jarivanu's people and that he disappeared. There's a lot of jungle between here and London. He could have died in any part of it."

"As for Atlantis," Manny said, "from what I saw this afternoon, the people who built this were not from some unknown continent. Nothing could vindicate Percy's theories. The man saw sixty-foot anacondas hanging from every bush. He was an incorrigible stretcher of the truth."

"He did have a bit of an overactive imagination," Christine said, giggling. "It's incredible to me that his real life wasn't romantic enough for him. He had to believe there was something totally fantastic around every corner."

"But Percy wasn't the only one with some mistaken notions. I blush to say it, Manny," she continued, "but until I heard you were Mayan, I thought they were an extinct people. It never occurred to me that any were still around."

"As you see, I am very much alive. And if you go to Mexico or Central America you will see Mayans all about you—driving taxis, working in shops, living their lives. But many people think as you do. We keep our language to ourselves, speaking Spanish to everyone else. And there is much about our past which is a mystery, so people have mythologized us and romanticized us, and made up all sorts of stories. But the reason for the mystery is plain. There is nothing supernatural about it.

"We now believe that at the time of the Spanish conquest, over sixty percent of all the people living in the great Mayan cities—Coba, Chichen Itza, Dzbilchaltan, and others—died. Some of these places contained over half a million inhabitants, and Spaniards introduced disease, most particularly smallpox. Many thousands also died from malnutrition and starvation, caused by the disruption of food growing and distribution centers.

"Most of the intellectuals, the artists, scribes, storytellers, dancers, and musicians lived in the cities, so most of them died. With them died the history of my people. You see, there is no great mystery attached to the disappearance of Mayan civilization. Human brutality and greed explain it quite nicely.

"But much of our past is being reclaimed. Great advances in translating the glyphs have been made and the door of the past is swinging wide open." He grinned, a little ruefully. Then he continued. "Actually, they present themselves as quite similar to us. Not all their troubles came from the Spaniards. At Copan, in the ninth century, so much of the forest was cut down to provide new lands for settlement and agriculture, for cooking fuel and building materials, that the entire valley was thrown out of ecological balance. There was extensive soil erosion and depletion, a decline in rainfall, and probably disease. Eventually, the city had to be abandoned.

"Also, it's beginning to seem as if my ancestors were rather bloodthirsty themselves. There seemed to be almost perpetual warfare and torture of prisoners." He waved an admonishing finger at them. "So, you'd better stay on my good side. I am not to be trifled with."

"That is all very nice, but how do we know this place is not cursed?" Raeder asked in a low voice.

Everyone stared at him. "Oh yes," he said angrily. "You are all so enlightened and scientific. But the natives are afraid and your so capable uncle and grandfather disappeared. Perhaps there are protections here to guard against unwelcome strangers. Remember what happened to the discoverers of King Tut's tomb. Perhaps these people also sought to protect their sacred places. You said yourself they could be violent and cruel." He shivered. "The vengeance of the dead is not to be scoffed at."

"You have seen too many horror movies. That story about Tut has been blown out of all proportion," Manny said scornfully. "I do not believe in curses or guardian mummies who have lived through the centuries. What do you think? There's some creature in there wrapped in moldy linen who'll kill us if we set foot inside?" He snorted. "That is all superstition. I have been present at many excavations, including the one at Copan. Am I not here to tell you about it?"

"Good, fine, you are so wise," Raeder said angrily. "I am going to bed. I do not wish to intrude on the discussion of such learned men." He stalked away.

"You shouldn't have made fun of him, Manny," Christine chided. "Lots of people believe in things like that. Raeder's not such a bad sort."

"He is being silly," Manny retorted. "We have no need of that. His fears are beginning to irk me. Being afraid of the Yanomani is one thing. They are a real people with a well-known inclination toward violence. Being afraid of shadows is something else again."

"Forget it," Tony said. "Raeder was hired as a cook and a guide. He's done his work. No one ever said part of his job was enthusiasm or a rational view of the universe. Let's not start cutting each other up now, after we've achieved so much."

"You are right, as usual, my friend," Manny

said. "I am a cantankerous old goat. I should have made love to one of those pretty Yanomani girls. Then I would be in a better mood. I found the matchstick girl to be especially lovely. Why should you be the only one known for his sexual appetites?"

Tony winced. "Thank God you kept your hands off her—you know perfectly well she's Jarivanu's wife. I doubt if making love to their chief warrior's woman is considered proper. The last thing we need is to offend them. I'd rather put up with your irritability." He stood up and stretched. "I'm off to bed. Wake me when your watch is up. Good night."

"I'll turn in, too," Christine said. "I'm exhausted. Be sure to rouse us if anything even the slightest bit suspicious happens. Don't be a hero, Manny."

He grinned at her, his white teeth glinting in the darkness. "I am brave, but I am not stupid. At the first sign of something going bump in the night, I will let you know. Good night, Christine."

He settled his back against a tree and rummaged through his pack. With a sigh of contentment, he pulled out his pipe, packed it with a particularly vile, strong tobacco, and puffed at it happily. His shotgun was at his side.

A full moon was up and some of its rays leaked through the canopy. The pyramid was visible in the darkness, more as a suggestion than a visible object. It stood as a bulk of shadows, too cohesive to be a random casting of light and light's absence.

"Where did you come from," Manny whispered into the darkness. "What other surprises can there be, besides the fact that you are here? Where did all those people go?"

He strained to hear anything unusual, but there was only the ordinary jungle sounds. He heard the insects' choruses, and the calls of animals on the hunt, and of those they hunted. It gave him a great feeling of peace. It was only in places like this that he felt fully alive.

Manny always believed that he visited a city, but he lived in the wilderness. The only time he felt true, gut-wrenching fear was when he contemplated the wilderness disappearing. Without it, he would be living the rest of his life in exile, his own home gone, destroyed.

No danger the jungle presented was as terrible as that. He had long reconciled himself to dying in the rain forest. At each corner, with every step, he said, "Is it you?" wondering if he would at last meet the death that waited for him—his special mistress. He looked forward to it with anticipation and dread intermingled. It was a delectable sensation and he savored it. When he had been swept away by the river, he had been certain his life was over. He recalled the feeling of calm that had settled over him. "So here it is at last," he had thought.

But he was still alive. Once more he was free to fantasize about his own end. Occasionally it occurred to him that he might die in a perfectly ordinary way—in a hospital bed, of old age—but it seemed an ignominious way to go. He had heard stories of men dying from sexual exhaustion. If he did die in bed, he felt that would be acceptable. Idly he wondered if, after he reached a ripe old age, he should arrange for it.

He flicked on his torch and stared up at the canopy of leaves. Perhaps this place was infested with poisonous spiders or snakes which sometimes attacked the careless. But he could see nothing. And that would only be an incident—it wouldn't happen enough times to start a legend.

As far as he knew, the Mayans never set booby traps to catch tomb robbers. Even if they did, the trap would only work once. Again, not enough to keep a legend alive for generations. Perhaps there were poisonous fumes that clouded the brain? Jarivanu had mentioned something about visions and madness.

Perhaps the place was similar to Delphi in Greece. Many thought the Delphic oracle was inspired by the vapors of the Cassotis, the spring which, according to some, ran through the temple. Plutarch wrote that the Pythia sometimes died from inhaling too many fumes when she was forced to receive Apollo's inspiration at an unpropitious time.

Could the pyramid had been built here because there was something that induced hallucinogenic visions? Could there be some sort of poisonous stream nearby?

Manny glanced at his watch. "How quickly the time passes," he thought. It was time to wake Tony. He contemplated for a brief moment letting him sleep, but dismissed the idea. Tony didn't need coddling, and tomorrow would be a busy day. He entered the hut.

"Wake my friend," he whispered, plucking at Tony's sleeve. Tony woke instantly.

"Everything all right?" Tony asked.

"Dismayingly peaceful. Not a ghost in sight. Not even a zombie or a vampire."

"I am disappointed," Tony said. "Give me the gun and get some sleep."

"You do not need to ask twice," Manny answered.

Tony went outside and settled by the fire. He watched as, gradually, the darkness faded into the pale light that meant the sun had risen. The pyramid stood out clearly. It was time to wake the others. "What an uneventful night," he thought. "Perhaps it's smooth sailing from now on."

In the daylight they could see that once there had been other buildings. Now, they were crumbled into ruins. Chunks of hewn stone were tumbled about the ground like a giant's toy blocks.

Stelae, carved with fantastic faces, rose about them, tilted at extreme angles or were completely overturned. Heads of gods and goddesses peered blankly into space; sacred birds and serpents stared, openmouthed, at the intruders.

Short hollow columns, which Manny said were used for the burnings of offerings, were very common. He recognized the face carved on them as that of Ch'ul, the deity who represented the sacredness of the universe.

The pyramid had been the focus of the small city. Manny pointed out shards of what looked like paving stone. "I think there were once roads leading to it," he said. "They've been destroyed long ago, of course, by the plants growing up from underneath, but you can see that this city was once laid out as a square, with a walkway from each corner pointing to the centerpiece, the pyramid."

Manny was fascinated by the stairway. It was covered with hieroglyphs and carvings. "Can you read any of it?" Christine asked.

"I think perhaps I can," he said. "At least enough to get some sense of how these buildings got here, and who built them.

"I believe these people left their home in flight from an invasion. Possibly, they mean the Spaniards. You can see the glyph for 'other' here and here," he said, pointing to them. "I don't think this means other Mayans.

"Many mighty warriors went on this journey. And this fellow, the tallest one, is the leader. See how he is portrayed in full warrior regalia. His headdress is the jaguar, which is a very prestigious symbol. Also, he is carrying a ceremonial rod with serpents. This, as well as his stature, identifies him as the ruler, the man with authority.

"Here are panels showing him with a lance and a shield, publicly displaying his prowess as a warrior. Also, here are pictures showing him surrounded by skulls and ropes for tying up victims for the sacrifice."

Christine shuddered. "They had human sacrifice?"

"Yes, we now think so. Prisoners of war were used and also commoners. For instance, in Copan, we found someone buried who we think was a scribe. Inside the tomb were remains of a bark-paper codex, paint pots filled with red pigment, and a pot decorated with the image of the patron god of scribes.

"His life was undemanding—there were no signs of arthritis or injury, although he must have been forty years old. Beside him was a boy. His teeth showed he suffered from ill health or poor nutrition. Most likely then, the boy was someone of no importance who was sacrificed so he might accompany the scribe into the underworld as his servant.

"The question is, why did these great warriors leave their homes and travel to this distant place? It was a fearsome journey. They brought with them many workers, priests, and scribes. An exodus was clearly their intention. They knew they were not coming back."

He stared at a series of glyphs, his lips pursed in thought. "I cannot make it out," he said finally. "They were protecting something of great value, but what, or where it is, I do not know. It must have meant much to them. Warriors did not normally run from an enemy."

"Do you think it could be up there?" Christine asked, pointing to the chamber at the top of the pyramid.

"It would seem likely. Of course, it is doubtless empty now, but perhaps there will be more writing describing what it was." His eyes gleamed. "I cannot wait until we return to London. What a tale this will be. Perhaps I shall head the expedition that comes here to excavate the site."

He called Tony and Raeder over. "We wish

to explore the room at the top. Will you come with us?''

"I wouldn't miss it for the world," Tony said. Raeder nodded in agreement.

"You feel better, eh?" Manny said, clapping him on the shoulder. "No more worries about curses?"

"In for a penny, in for a pound," Raeder said with a shrug.

"A good, fatalistic attitude." He grabbed his gun and started up the stairs. "First floor," he called cheerfully. "Ladies underwear, negligees, marital aids."

Christine glanced at Tony and burst out laughing. "If this is how we begin, what do you think is at the top?"

"Harems and odalisques, no doubt," Tony said. He took her hand. "Up we go."

They took their time, moving slowly, watching their step. Tony cautioned Manny, who was desperate to race to the top, "These stairs are steep. We can't risk an injury. The room's been there for hundreds of years. It won't vanish in fifteen minutes."

"You are so calm, Tony. Is it your English blood that makes you so unflappable?"

"Actually, I think it was my exposure to H. Rider Haggard books as a boy. I modeled myself as a character from his stories. It was during my period as a suffering youth. I strove for an appearance of great inner pain controlled only by tight-lipped fortitude and an iron will."

"You had a sad childhood?" Manny asked, with sympathy in his voice.

"No, not at all. But at twelve I went around pretending I had suffered a terrible misfortune. I would stare off into space and murmur things like, 'Of course, what does life hold for me now,' and give great, bronchitic sighs. My mother told me I sounded like an old bellows. She also told me if I didn't stop, she'd burn my library card."

Manny laughed. "You were a romantic. That is very nice. It explains many things."

"You aren't very romantic with me," Christine complained. "You never go around brooding about me."

"I never had to—you're a real person. I brooded about slender, mysterious women with Slavic accents and high cheekbones who undulated across balconies wearing diaphanous gowns. They were running away from palace intrigues and brutal husbands. Quite often I saved them."

"But not always?"

"No," Tony sighed. "Sometimes they were murdered before I could get to them. That's when I would mope around the house and tell my parents I wanted to renounce the world. I kept threatening to either run away and become a monk or go off to Africa to find King Solomon's mines. My father finally offered to send me one day.

"I was always extremely indignant whenever they asked me to do something mundane like run to the grocer's for a jar of marmalade. It hardly seemed the thing to ask of a man who has looked death in the face a thousand times without flinching."

"You must have been insufferable."

"All children are insufferable."

"According to my mother, I was an absolute angel," Christine said smugly.

Tony looked at her reproachfully. "Christine! You know perfectly well Lily thought you were a holy terror. You shouldn't go around making up fables. She once told me that if the little princes in the tower had been anything like you, she didn't blame Richard a bit."

"Mother tends to exaggerate things," Christine muttered. "Look," she said brightly, changing the subject, "we're almost at the top."

Manny had reached the stone chamber at the top of the pyramid. An open doorway, framed by carved columns, led inside. He peered in, but it was too dark to see anything. "I am going in," he said to the others. "Follow me." He turned on his torch and crossed through the entrance. A few steps behind him was Raeder, then Christine and Tony.

"Well, I'll be damned," Manny whispered.

The room was small and shaped like a pentagon. A shelf was in each corner and on four of the shelves were skulls that seemed to be made of glass. They glittered dully in the torchlight. Cautiously, Tony picked one up. He saw that it was not glass but crystal. It looked like it had been carved from a single block of quartz. The eye sockets were empty. The mouth gave back a toothy, translucent grin.

"I have seen an identical one in Mexico City," Manny said breathlessly.

"What does it mean?" Christine asked him.

"I don't know. The arguments about the crystal skulls has gone on for many years. No one knows who made them or if they are a contemporary hoax." He looked around the room. "I think we can safely say the theory that they are fakes can be put to rest."

He walked over to the empty shelf. "I wonder if the skull in Mexico belongs here?" He thought for a moment. "That cannot be," he said finally, answering his own question. "That would mean others had been here. Still, there is plainly a relationship."

Raeder shivered. "I do not like this room. What can a skull mean but death?"

"You don't like anything," Manny retorted. "You stumble on a miracle and you are ready to wet your pants."

Raeder looked sulky. "So what was this room used for? You who are so smart you lecture and treat us like children, you tell me."

"How should I know," Manny muttered. "I'm a knowledgeable layman, not an archaeologist. I have never seen a room like this before. When we return to London, I shall get funding for the Manuel Aburto expedition, and come back and resolve all the mysteries. Perhaps the hieroglyphics explain it. I cannot read them all."

"Is that what you're planning?" Christine asked. "It seems exciting."

"Of course it is exciting. And you shall come back here with me. We shall all be a team—no, a family, like brothers and sister." Manny clapped his hands together, clasping one in the other. The world changed.

The sun darkened. Clouds turned black and streamed across the sky, pushed by the violent wind. He paused, sniffing the air. There was a disturbance. Somewhere an animal screamed, its bellow echoing through the valley. It was frightened.

Intruders were coming. It had been so long, he thought he was safe. He had let down his guard. Now, he must hurry to the gateway. This world was so fragile—it could not survive alien incursions.

Before he had found this land, it had been a dumb place, innocent of consciousness. He alone had invested it with meaning. Now, it was a mirror reflecting only him. It was the image of his mind, and he would allow it to show no other face.

He muttered to himself as he loped along the ground. There were no words, only gutteral sounds of anger. He had not needed words for a very long time now. A more perfect understanding was possible in this place. The world was his creation, always in harmony with its creator's thoughts. Thinking and being had become one.

Fumbling at his side, he found the knife. It was important to kill them quickly, before they dirtied this virgin place. In this paradise he was the angel at the gate with the flaming sword, as well as the ruler and designer of all things. None could enter.

Only a few ever escaped him. But they had

gone mad, gibbering with fear at what they saw. He sent them to their own place. They never returned. Others he killed, if he was in the mood. Their carcasses he let rot in the sun, to be fought over by scavengers. A few he let escape to wander and meet their fate at the hands of some nightmare. He would decide the fate of these new ones at the moment he saw them. He liked to look at their faces first. One way or another, they would be punished.

8

The floor spun away, the walls exploded. They were engulfed in a swirl of motion. Light flashed and a blue sky erupted into view. Somewhere, something was screaming. Waves of nausea welled up from their guts and they all vomited.

Gasping, dazed, they looked up into a hot, orange sun. "Mother of God," Raeder cried out. "It is an earthquake." He panicked and tried to run, but Tony grabbed him around the waist. "Let me go," Raeder screamed, twisting and thrashing.

"There's nowhere to go," Tony shouted. "Calm down. It's not an earthquake."

Raeder's knees buckled. Tony gently let him sag to the ground. "What is happening?" he groaned. "Where are we?"

"Damned if I know," Tony said, looking around. "But I don't think we're in Kansas anymore, Toto."

"What the hell are you talking about?" Raeder snarled. "Who's Toto? We were never in Kansas. Have you lost your mind?"

"Are you all right, Chris?" Tony asked, putting his arms around her. She was staring around, stupefied. She nodded, swallowing hard.

He took her by the shoulders and turned her to face him. "Say something," he demanded.

"What happened?"

"I don't know."

"Terrific. Have we concluded this conversation?"

He kissed her. "You're wonderful, Chris."

"I know that," she said, with real irritation in her voice. "This hardly seems the time to be mouthing platitudes, Tony."

Tony looked at Manny and shrugged. Manny shrugged back. "I take it you're fine?" Tony asked him.

"I am fine, but I do not understand. Where the hell are we? What happened?"

Tony shook his head slowly. "We were standing in that little room and then . . . presto." Bewildered, he looked at the strange hills that surrounded them. There was no sign of the Mayan city or their camp.

He hefted his shotgun. "At least this came with us. What else have we got?"

Manny answered, "The torches, our guns, some cartridges. We each have knives. Christine's got her Polaroid. I've got a packet of meat . . . that's about it. It's just what we took into the temple. We never intended to leave camp." Manny looked around again. "Have any of you ever seen trees like this?"

The trees' trunks were curved into gentle arches, their bark marked with a coarse diamond pattern. Instead of leaves, there were large fronds, each approximately three feet long, covered in prickles.

Tony said, "They're a bit like trees I've seen in Florida. And look at these ferns all over the ground." He kicked at the undergrowth. "This is simply not the rain forest of Brazil. We're in a totally different place. I don't understand it, but I can't draw any other conclusion."

"You know what it reminds me of?" Christine asked. Manny and Tony looked at her. "Promise you won't laugh," she said.

"Spit it out, Chris. This is no time for games," Tony said impatiently.

"Some movies I've seen," she said reluctantly.

"What movies?" Tony demanded. "Where do you think we are? Hollywood?"

"We could be for all I know. But this place looks like the backdrop for several big lizard films I've wasted precious moments of my life watching." Despite her flippant words, her voice was tight and frightened.

"I do not understand you," Manny said, looking very puzzled. "What is a big lizard film?"

"Oh, you know, people go through a crack in the earth, or they're in a balloon that's blown off course, and they end up in some place filled with gila monsters that have frills pasted onto their backs—dinosaurs, all that. There's always this sort of greenery. Also, I think I remember seeing something like this at the Natural History Museum, when Tony and I went there. They had a gallery of dinosaurs and it had a few dioramas. Remember, Tony?" He looked at her incredulously. Manny plainly doubted her sanity.

"It was just a thought," she said feebly. "After all, Percy was always looking for a lost world. Remember the Conan Doyle story." She looked first at Tony, then at Manny. "Forget it," she said. "Just forget I said anything."

"I told you the place was cursed," Raeder said vehemently. "We are being punished for violating their temple. The earth has swallowed us up. You would not listen—now we are in Hell."

Tony ignored him. "Chris," he said faintly, "do you remember that dinosaur bone you found in your grandfather's trunk? Remember how the doctor said it wasn't anywhere near old enough—that it was some sort of hoax?" Christine's eyes widened.

"What is all this?" Manny demanded. "What bone, what hoax?"

Together, Tony and Christine told him the story. "It was really the beginning of this expedition," Christine said. "I was looking for an excuse to do something different . . . something that would prove I wasn't just a layabout.

"I got all excited about finding this odd bone and then, when it seemed like it was a fake because it was clearly of rather recent manufacture, I went through a terrible letdown." She shrugged. "I wanted something magical and extraordinary in my life very badly and it brought back stories about Grandfather so I decided to retrace his footsteps. Now that I think of it, none of it makes any sense."

"I think I understand," Manny said. "After

all, I have spent much of my life avoiding the ordinary and so has Tony. Of course," he said, looking around, "this does seem to be a bit extreme."

"I wonder if that bone really was a fake," Tony said. "Do you think Percy actually found some sort of hidden world filled with prehistoric animals?"

"Tony," Christine said nervously, "do you remember Dr. Langley telling us that bone belonged to a *Tyrannosaurus rex*?"

"Shit," Tony said in a very heartfelt manner. He looked at his shotgun.

"Would that kind of gun be any good against it?" Christine asked.

"It might use it as a toothpick after dinner," he said, feeling a little sick. "I'd rather not discuss what's on the menu."

"Those are the really big ones, aren't they?" Manny asked. Christine and Tony nodded. "With the teeth and the little arms in front?" he continued, looking at them intently, holding his arms in front of him like a dog begging. They nodded again. "We've got to get out of here," he said.

"But where is here?" Raeder demanded. "How do we get back when we don't know where we are?"

They all looked at each other. "I'm scared," Christine said flatly.

Suddenly, Tony tensed. He motioned everyone to be quiet. "I'm sure I felt something— some sort of tremor," he whispered. They all froze. In the distance, they heard a rumble like thunder.

"Do you think there's a storm coming?" Christine asked, looking into the sky. It was a limpid blue.

"That was never thunder," Manny said. "Something's moving. A lot of somethings. It sounds like a herd of animals—big ones."

"Quick, everyone get up on that knoll, behind the trees," Tony ordered. He shoved them roughly toward cover.

The wind changed, bringing with it a rank, heavy, animal odor. The smell made them cough a little and they covered their mouths to muffle the noise. Tony pushed them farther back, away from the noise which had taken on the heavy, pounding sound of pistons moving in a powerful machine.

Cautiously, they looked down and saw the fronds part. For an instant, Christine convinced herself she was seeing a small group of rhinoceroses push their way into the clearing. Her mind was trying to force the extraordinary sight into an acceptable, if puzzling, image. It was a brave effort, but doomed to failure.

A group of gigantic, horned reptiles were feeding placidly on the trees' leaves. The adults looked, to her stunned eyes, to be about thirty feet long from their beaked snouts to the tips of their tails. They seemed about ten feet high at the shoulder. A pair of long, sharp horns projected from their foreheads, while a short horn projected from their snouts. A thick, frilled plate lay over their necks. Dull gray-green in color, they blended in surprisingly well with the trees and vegetation.

The smallest—the young—stayed close to the

center of the herd while the largest, which
Christine assumed were male, stood on the
outskirts, guarding the females and the infants.

It was, she thought, stifling an hysterical gig-
gle, a classic scene of pastoral tranquility. Paint-
ings very similar in nature with titles like
"Noontide Peace" and "The Haven of the
Herd" adorned many drawing rooms. They, of
course, substituted some picturesque cows of
the Channel Island persuasion for the giant
reptiles; but, for all intents and purposes, the
subject matter was much the same.

She leaned toward Tony and whispered, "I
know it's silly, since this is only a dream and
not really happening, but I think I'm going to
scream."

"Don't you dare, because if you do, I'll feed
you to one of those things. What the hell are
they, besides large?"

"I believe they're *Triceratops*," she said,
numbly. "They seem to be vegetarians, if that's
any consolation."

"Not much."

"They are monsters," Raeder whispered. "If
these are the animals, then what are the people
like? Are they giants, too?"

"I doubt if there are any people," Christine
said. "These things lived well before people—
in our world, at any rate. Unless of course, we
really are on a Hollywood set. In that case, Ra-
quel Welch should pop out at any moment
now."

Manny tugged at her sleeve. "Christine," he
whispered, "take a picture. No one's ever going to believe this. I want objective proof."

"Good idea. I'd like some objective proof myself." She raised the camera and clicked the shutter. There was a burst of brilliant light—the flash had gone off.

The animals wheeled and bellowed in a complete panic. The largest male, angry and aggressive, spotting the intruders on the knoll, pawed the ground very much like an enraged bull. Then he charged toward them, his horns lowered.

Everything happened in the wink of an eye, and everything happened as slowly as if they were underwater, moving through a medium that resisted every movement.

Sounds assaulted them—the screams of the animals, the pounding of their clawed feet, the snorting, rank breath of the bull—all drenching them in rhythms of chaos and fear.

It seemed impossible for something so immense to move so quickly. They stared at the violent black streak racing to meet them. Then, the blur defined itself. The cruel horns glinted in the bright sun. The mouth snapped open and shut like a turtle's. And, in the middle of all this fury were the tiny eyes, cold and expressionless.

Manny fired the shotgun. The explosion echoed in their ears. The animal slowed, startled and afraid. Manny fired again and he bellowed, wheeled, and ran. The herd, taking its cue from the leader, retreated. Then they were gone, leaving only the trampled ground as evidence that they had ever been there.

Tony grabbed Manny and hugged him. "You

saved us, you lecherous bastard. We'd have been dead if it weren't for you."

Manny shrugged. "It was nothing." He was trembling.

Christine was laughing and crying at the same time. "How did you know it would work?"

"I didn't. It was the only thing I could think of to do. Frankly, I was not sanguine. I am very surprised to be alive."

"I'll bet this is the first time anyone's fired a gun here," Tony said. "I don't think this place is big on technology."

"Did you get the picture, Christine?" Manny asked.

"I . . . oh, dear . . ." She pointed at the undeveloped negative lying on the ground. It was completely smeared, except for the distinct mark of a muddy boot heel.

"Ah, well," Manny sighed. "There will be other chances."

"God, I hope not," Christine said fervently.

Sitting on the ground, Raeder looked at them with blank eyes. Gingerly, he moved his hands over his body, assuring himself that he was alive and in one piece. For the first time in many years, he whispered a prayer.

Manny overheard the mumbled words and looked down at him. "I did not know you are a religious man."

"I am a practical man. We need help. I do not care where it comes from. We are in no position to overlook anything." He wiped sweat from his forehead.

Overhead, they heard a shrill cry. They

looked up and saw a large leather-winged creature gliding in the clear blue sky. As it caught each updraft, it rose high and then swooped down again toward the ground. A long, bony crest extended several feet beyond the back of its skull. When it came in close view, Tony saw its huge wingspread and the large, wickedly pointed beak.

"Ever seen *that* in *King Kong?*" he asked Christine, trying to sound jovial.

"Something very like it," she answered soberly. "It almost carried off the heroine for brunch." She looked at the flying reptile. "It looks a little like a pterodactyl."

Moodily, Tony shielded his eyes and stared off into the distance. He badly wanted to see something that would assure him of his sanity.

"You know what's odd?" Christine asked.

"Odd? Why no, whatever strikes you as odd?" he said bitterly. "Everything strikes me as perfectly normal."

Ignoring his tone, she said, "I think it must mean something that these animals are so familiar. After all, if we'd somehow been transported to Mars, wouldn't we be seeing sentient vegetables or creatures with three heads?"

"I suppose," Tony said. "Shall we take as a working assumption that we are on the planet Earth, although we don't know where?"

"Or when," Christine added.

Everyone looked at her. "It does look a bit prehistoric," she said hesitantly. Tony shut his eyes for a moment. He was getting a headache.

Slowly he opened them, half hoping he would wake up in his own apartment, in his

own bed. The unbroken view of hills and trees
presented itself again. Then he started. There
was a break in the pattern. On the side of the
hill opposite, against a jumble of rock, was a
tumbled pile of branches. It had an oddly struc-
tured look to it, as if the crisscrossing of wood
and leaves was not totally random. There was
a hint of ruin about it and of abandoned intent.

"Manny, what do you think of that over
there against the stones?" He directed Manny's eyes to the huddle of sticks and fronds.

For a moment, Manny was utterly still. Then
he looked hard at Tony. "Someone built that,"
he said flatly.

Raeder and Christine craned their necks, trying to see. "Let's go," Tony said. "If there are
other people here, we've got to find them. We
need answers." Without another word, they
started down the hill.

It was a hut. The roof had fallen in and the
walls were collapsed, but there was no mistak-
ing its purpose.

"Look here," Manny said, showing them the
end of one of the branches. "This was cut by a
knife." Close to the entrance was a blackened
circle of stones.

"I don't think this has been abandoned for
too long," Tony said. "Otherwise, it'd be overgrown and animals would have disturbed and
trampled it." He stirred up the ashes in the fire
pit. "We have company," he said slowly. "I'm
relieved, but we need to be cautious. We don't
know anything about them except that they're
armed with knives and know what fire is. We

could be talking about anything from a caveman to someone just like ourselves.''

He paused to gather his thoughts. ''Let's try
to resurrect this old shelter for tonight. I don't
want to risk any more exploring. I think we've
all had more than enough surprises for one day.
If someone else has stayed here, perhaps it
means this is a relatively safe place to be.
Manny and I will take turns standing guard
during the night.

''Tomorrow, we'll have to find water and get
some food. Hopefully, there's something living
here that isn't Godzilla's great-grandmother.
Then, we'll try to find our mysterious companion.'' He looked around. ''Unless there are any
comments, let's get our house in order.''

Silently, they set about their work. All of
them felt exhausted and numb, uncertain of
what lay before them. Christine gathered fuel
for the fire, piling up in separate heaps small
twigs, dried pieces of moss, and thicker
branches. Many of them she found lying close
to the fire ring. She was grateful. She had no
intentions of wandering away from camp.

Occasionally overhead, they would see the
winged beasts circling in the air and hear their
harsh cries. Once, Raeder pointed out to Manny
a creature on a distant hill with a sinuous, serpentine neck, moving along the ridge. They
were too far away to see it in better detail.

As the sun sank low in the sky, they began
to get cold. Christine built up the fire and they
huddled around it, holding their hands out to
it, partially to warm them, partially as a gesture
of inclusion. The flames were the only point of

familiarity in this alien landscape. All of them felt unutterably lonely.

They gnawed on the strips of tapir meat, trying to make them last. The flesh was dry and tasteless. Trying to raise her spirits, Christine threw a few more pieces of moss and twigs into the fire. It blazed up for a moment, then subsided. The moss gave off a sickly sweet odor as it burned.

The smell made her sleepy and lethargic. She leaned against Tony, taking comfort from the warmth of his body close to hers. He muttered something. His words were slurred and unintelligible.

"What was that, darling?" she tried to say, but it was difficult. Mouth, tongue, and jaw moved far too slowly. Time stretched like a rubber band pulled to its extremes. To her own ears, her words sounded like a record played at the wrong speed. Each syllable dragged out into infinity.

Searching for some point of stability, she reached out to touch Tony's shoulder. Her arm melted, ran, and stretched. Its bones dissolved and it had no more solidity than a piece of hot wax. She stared as her fingers lengthened and sprouted like creeping vines. The tendrils wriggled along the ground and began burrowing into the soil. Sickly pale as worms, they dug deep, unearthing slugs and hardshelled insects that scuttled over her legs, their pincers clacking.

Overhead, the stars cartwheeled slowly in the sky, leaving behind them streaks of flame. Then they winked out, one by one. Darkness folded in on itself, turning, rotating, sucking away the air.

Gasping for breath, Christine tried to stand but the ground warped away and there was nothing solid left in the world. She stumbled. Somewhere, there was laughter.

Suddenly, she bent double as though someone had punched her in the stomach. She retched. Her gut contracted violently. Her legs collapsed under her and she vomited again. Through the haze of nausea she saw reality reassert itself. The world re-formed and solidified. She recognized the others and saw they were in the same condition as herself.

Manny staggered to his feet and stomped out the fire. He stood there, his chest heaving, his eyes wild. "It is the moss," he gasped. "The fumes must be toxic."

Tony bent over and helped Christine to her feet. "Sweetheart, are you all right?" Gently, he brushed back the hair from her face.

Unexpectedly, she felt shy. "I must be a mess," she said, turning her head away.

"You're beautiful," he said gently. "You're the most beautiful woman in the world. I love you." He kissed her forehead.

"We're all right, too," Manny said, grinning.

"I'm not," Raeder muttered. "Never have I experienced such nightmares. My hands got up and walked away on their own, taking my arms with them, my feet went in another direction with my legs. I lay there a torso, screaming."

"Ah, my friend," Manny said, clapping him on the back, "so long as you retained your manhood, nothing else matters." He patted his crotch.

"You are obsessed," Raeder said sulkily.

Christine's eyes began to get heavy. She was very tired. She leaned heavily against Tony. Manny smiled at her. "Get to sleep, all of you. I will keep first watch." Tony opened his mouth to protest, but Manny cut him off. "I am fine. But if I see anyone, I intend on asking them why they burn that moss. I wonder if this is a prehistoric opium den."

Manny kept watch under a sky littered with stars he couldn't identify. The heavens were as unfamiliar to him as everything else here. A few times during the night he was certain someone was watching him. The hairs on the back of his neck prickled. He wheeled around, trying to catch sight of the prowler, but there was nothing. Nervously, he stood guard until he felt his eyes begin to close. Then he woke Tony to take his place. He threw himself onto the ground and fell instantly into a deep, dreamless sleep.

He watched them from the shadows. They were doing well. But he would soon have to kill them. They were trying to re-create this mute world, force it into the mold their own minds desired. Their words spoiled a place that knew nothing of symbols or abstractions, but simply existed without contradiction, without thought. Only he could translate between mind and act. There could be no rival world-shapers. When they were gone, he could again sink into the silence of pure being. They would be gone soon. He would see to it himself, if he had to. But the woman reminded him of something.

The next morning, Tony and Manny looked briefly for signs of an intruder but could find nothing. Tony decided to continue the search later. Finding food was their first priority. They were all hungry and thirsty.

"I think there must be water close by," Manny said. "No one puts shelter far from water. Also, the ground here is damp from underneath. This is not dew."

"Let's go," Tony said. "We'll try downhill. Keep on the alert. God knows what we'll run across."

They marched in single file, Tony in the lead, Manny bringing up the rear. They jumped at each cracking twig, at the rustling leaves. The ground became softer, squelching under their feet. They followed a gentle incline and came to a large pond at its base.

Manny bent down and took a tiny sip of water, swirling it around in his mouth as if it were a fine wine. "It is sweet," he said. "It smells fresh." He shrugged. "I think we have to take our chances. If it is as pristine here as it seems, the water should be pure."

He cupped his hands and scooped up the water. He drank deeply, wiping his mouth. He said, "It's much better than London tap water."

That was good enough. They all began to drink.

Raeder dipped his head close to the pond, then yanked it back. He was looking straight into two tiny eyes, widely spaced, peering at him from the water. He retreated from the edge.

"What is it?" Tony asked. Raeder pointed. Something brown, and of indeterminate size was swimming close to the bank. Two large, clawed feet planted themselves on the bank. Fourteen feet away, a spiked tail moved lazily in the water. Heaving itself onto the mud, something that looked very like a turtle blinked and gaped.

Wattles hung on either side of the massive neck, creased with deep wrinkles, laden with warts. Two cowlike horns sprouted from the base of the skull. Its shell, perched well back, rose in three separate ridges. Very slowly, the animal straightened its legs and began to pull itself up out of the pond.

"Dinner," Manny breathed. "Many dinners." Carefully, he reached for his shotgun and aimed it at the turtle's head. The turtle yawned and pulled its head into its shell.

"Why does life conspire to make me ridiculous at a moment like this?" Manny demanded, raising his fist toward heaven. "Is there no dignity inherent in existence?"

"Could we discuss metaphysics some other time?" Christine said irritably. "Like when we get back to the twentieth century? Existentialism seems a bit out of place here."

"Tip it on its back," Raeder said. "At least it won't get away."

"Good idea," Tony said. They gathered on one side of the turtle and, with a grunt, heaved. The shell lifted a few inches from the ground, then dropped back. It was incredibly heavy. The turtle poked its head out, looked around disapprovingly, then retreated back into its shell.

Tony jumped up and started hacking at a tree, snapping off heavy branches. "Don't let that thing move if it gets any ideas," he yelled. "I'll get some levers."

Manny crawled on top of the shell and sat on it. The turtle, who had plainly had enough, stuck out its head and legs and started to crawl to the water. "Get the gun," Manny shouted to Raeder. "Shoot it, shoot it."

Raeder snatched up the shotgun and fired. The turtle's head blew apart. Manny was splattered with blood, bone and brain.

"Shit," Christine said, turning away. She fought to keep from being sick. Manny rolled off into the mud. "Good shot," he said. He pulled out his knife.

They butchered the turtle, scooping out the meat and wrapping it in fronds. Using the shell to hold it, they pushed it back toward camp, shoving it up the hill.

"Look up there," Raeder said, pointing to the sky. A pterodactyl, spotting the fresh meat, was circling lazily around them. It rose up higher, a diminishing speck in the crystal clear sky, then dived, claws extended.

A rush of wind blew them back and the leather wings beat about their heads. Christine was knocked to the ground. Screaming, the animal tried to drive them off, its claws raking at their faces, its long, wicked beak snapping open and shut.

Tony hit its head with the gun butt, but it only bounced off the bony crest. Another slash of its claws sliced open his arm. He screamed.

An answering cry came from across the hills. The pterodactyl rose suddenly in the air, dropping a piece of meat it had seized. It flew upwards, joining others of its kind that had suddenly appeared in the sky. They wheeled once, then, in a burst of speed, sped away.

The ground was swarming with tiny, green lizards racing through the undergrowth. They scrabbled over rock and through the ferns. Some climbed trees and disappeared among the leaves.

A shattering cry echoed among the hills. The air quivered with the reverberations. And then the ground began to shake, in response to some steady, rhythmic, disturbance.

A few hundred feet from them, the herd of *Triceratops* galloped, racing across the plain. They were being driven, herded like cattle. Their pursuer was close behind. No one had to ask what it was—they all recognized a *Tyrannosaurus rex*.

Bent over so that its upper body was parallel to the ground, its legs a blurred suggestion of muscle and claw, it looked like a weapon, hurled on its deadly trajectory by some unseen, powerful hand.

The rows of glittering teeth gave the face the appearance of a grinning skull. Saliva dripped from the open mouth. It was a nightmare come to life, radiating menace and death. Its victim was close at hand.

Lagging toward the back of the herd, one *Tri-*

ceratops was clearly weaker than the others. It stumbled once and its enemy raked at it with a clawed hind foot. Shocked into desperate action, the *Triceratops* wheeled, lowered its head and charged, gouging a hole in the *Tyrannosaurus*'s upper leg.

It howled once, then stooped and closed its jaws on the back of the animal's neck. There was a scream and a plainly audible crack as the plate at the base of the skull broke. Then the spine snapped. The *Triceratops* went down, its legs kicking frantically, still trying to run. A shudder ran through its entire body, its eyes rolled back, and then it was still.

The *Tyrannosaurus* ripped out a hunk of flesh and stood upright, fresh blood dripping from its mouth onto the ground. It stood taller than many of the trees. The tiny eyes surveyed the landscape, looking for challengers to its kill. Then it bent down again toward the carcass.

"Let's get the hell out of here," Christine whispered. Raeder, who looked like a shock victim, nodded his head vehemently. They took as many pieces of meat as they could carry and slowly, freezing at the slightest noise, backed away.

After what seemed an eternity, they got back to the hut. "Let's see your arm," Manny said to Tony. "What did that overgrown vulture do to you?"

"It's nothing," Tony said. He looked at the long shallow gash that ran along his forearm. "It's not deep."

"We've got to clean it," Manny said. "Who knows what kind of infection you can get. Who knows what kind of filth was on those talons."

Christine paled. "Do you think it's serious?"

Manny shrugged. "I just wish we had our medical kit. I'd feel a lot better if we could disinfect the wound." He looked at Christine. "Build up the fire. I'll be back."

"Where are you going?" Tony demanded.

"To get some water. Get that fire going."

Walking as quietly as he could, he returned to where they'd abandoned the shell and the rest of the meat. He could see the pterodactyls gathering and swooping down toward the *Triceratop's* carcass. The *Tyrannosaurus* was stooped over the body. Occasionally, it raised its head and snapped at the scavengers. Manny's heart rose into his mouth.

Dragging the shell back to the pond, he filled it with water. Then, as quietly as he could, carefully pushed it back to the hut. "I feel like Robinson Crusoe," he muttered. "And I don't like it. Why the hell couldn't I have brought my water bottle? And where's Friday when you need him?"

When he returned, he saw that the fire was blazing. He looked at Tony, who nodded. He looked pale. Manny said to him, "You know we've got to do this?"

"I know. Let's get it over with."

"Do what?" Christine demanded, sounding frightened. "What's happening?"

"We can't let the wound turn septic," Tony

said to her, as gently as he could. "We've got to clean it as best we can."

"Do you want me to hold you?" Raeder said.

"I think you'd better," Tony answered. He lay down on the ground.

"Holding Tony is my department," Christine said, completely confused.

"You take my left hand, Chris," Tony said, holding it out to her. Raeder got on his knees and pressed down on Tony's shoulders.

"Here," Manny said, rolling up his hat. "Put this between your teeth." Then he took out his knife and held it in the fire.

"Oh, my God, you're not serious," Christine gasped. "Stop it, I won't let . . ."

Swiftly, Manny bent down and laid the hot metal against the wound. There was a smell of hair and flesh burning. Tony bucked and writhed. His back arched. Manny took the knife away and gently wiped the beads of sweat from Tony's face.

"I had to cauterize it," he said to Christine. He thought she was going to faint. "I'm sorry, there was no other way." She was too numb to answer.

Tony sat up, then bent over, putting his head between his legs. After a moment he looked up again. "Thought I was going to black out," he said sheepishly. "It hurts like hell."

"You will be all right," Manny said. "It will make a very distinctive scar and impress all the women." Tony managed a faint grin.

"Bathe the arm," Manny said to Christine.

He took off his shirt and ripped it into strips. "Use this to bandage it. I never liked this shirt anyways. It's not my color."

With shaking hands, she followed his instructions. "If we don't get out of here soon," she thought, "we're going to die."

9

He moved quietly, ducking behind rocks, peering out from behind trees. Tonight, he would kill them. There was no help for it. He could allow no pretenders, no challengers. It was kill or be killed. Of course they wanted his world—he didn't blame them. Such a treasure, such a prize. Here a man could be a god—the only conscious being in a world of unthinking brutes. Without him, everything would disappear.

There was a guard sitting by the fire. He would kill him first, then go inside and kill the others. Then he could have their clothes. It was a pity about the woman, but there it was. Still, it was odd how she seemed to remind him of something.

"Ring around the rosy," he muttered. "Pocketful of posy. One, two, three, and they all fall down." That was a magic charm. It protected him and made him strong. Someone important had taught it to him long ago and now it kept him safe from danger. He frowned. No one had taught him anything. He was alone here. It was his magic. He must have created it so long ago he couldn't remember doing it. That was true of many things.

Slowly, he began crawling on his belly toward the hut. His teeth were bared and he flexed his long, strong fingers. The man seemed lost in thought, unaware of anything unusual. It would be simple. He sprang forward and on top of him.

Manny shouted. The face of a fierce animal was thrust into his. Fingers curled around his throat and squeezed. Manny thrashed, trying to throw off the creature that gripped him. There was an explosion inside his head and red streaks of light clouded his eyes. He heard footsteps and Tony yelling. The weight on his chest lifted.

Manny staggered to his feet, gasping for breath. Tony and Raeder held grimly onto a twisting, shrieking figure that snapped at them very much like a dog trying to bite. To his astonishment, Manny realized it was a human being—an old man.

He was almost naked, wearing only a few bits of hide held up with vines. Every inch of wrinkled, withered skin was deeply tanned, including his lips. His long hair and beard were wildly tangled with leaves and sticks. Pitifully thin, his eyes bloodshot and rolling in their sockets, he looked like the poor demented creatures Manny had seen in carnivals who were advertised as wild men.

"Calm down," Tony shouted. "Stop struggling. We're not going to hurt you." The old man screeched and spat. He raked the air with long, filthy nails.

"Please stop," Christine said, coming up to him. "We really mean you no harm."

"I'm not so sure of that," Manny said grimly. "That bastard tried to kill me. I wouldn't mind giving him a kick. Anyway, what makes you think he speaks English?"

Christine looked at him in exasperation. "You're not to lay a hand on him. The poor thing's frightened out of his wits." Manny snorted.

"Look, here's some food," she said, turning back to the captive. She held out a piece of roasted turtle meat.

The old man sniffed at it and eyed her warily. Suddenly, he snatched it from her hand and shoved it whole into his mouth. He chewed it furiously.

"Maybe he's just hungry," Christine said sympathetically. She got another piece of meat. This time, he took it more slowly, pausing to stare at her face. He made an odd, gutteral noise.

"Did you speak?" she asked eagerly. She looked at Tony. "Should we let him go?"

"Certainly not," Tony said. "For one thing, he may know something. For another, he's a damn homicidal maniac. We can't let him roam around loose. He'll bolt as soon as I release him."

The old man twisted his head around and snarled at Tony.

"Can you understand me at all?" Christine asked. "Oh, if only you could tell me your name." She pursed her lips in thought. "I know," she said, struck with inspiration. Patting her chest, she said, "Christine." She looked anxiously into the old man's face, and nodded encouragingly. "Chris-tine," she said again, this time very slowly.

A look of recognition brightened his features. Heartened, Christine pointed to him. The old man straightened. In a voice as cracked and squeaky as a gate that had been shut for years, he said with an impeccable British accent, "God."

They looked at each other in astonishment. "He can understand us," Christine said excitedly.

"He's a loony," Raeder said disconsolately.

"Shut up," Christine snapped. "We're making progress."

"Cetainly," Tony said. "We know we need a psychiatrist and a couple of vials of Thorazine."

"Maybe he's telling the truth," Manny offered. "Personally, I find it quite plausible that the universe is run by a half-mad lunatic."

Christine scowled at him. "You're no help. None of you are." Hesitantly, she took the man's hand. He snatched it away. She smiled at him encouragingly. "God?" she repeated in a questioning tone, pointing to him. He nodded emphatically.

"How long have you been here?" she asked, again spacing out the words so that they came slowly.

"Forever," he said calmly. His voice seemed

a little less rusty. Frowning with concentration, he added, "Get out."

"Friendly place," Manny said. "They certainly do know how to make a person feel welcome." He leaned toward the man. "Do you have any young daughters?"

"Manny!" Christine said, outraged. "This is no time for stupid jokes."

"Who's joking?" Manny asked.

"Sod off," the old man said violently.

Manny said, "I think he understands more than he lets on. Think of what this means, Christine, if we ever get back home. You could bring back a dinosaur and an English-speaking caveman with a violent temper who claims he's God and has a taste for obscenities. No one will ever forget the Fawcett expedition, I promise you that."

The old man's head jerked up. He stared at Manny. "Fawcett?" he repeated. "Fawcett, Fawcett," he muttered the name over and over again.

"I'm Christine Fawcett," Christine said, softly. "Does that name mean something to you?" She looked hard at the man, trying to understand the expression on his face.

His eyes widened again. "Jack," he said slowly, as if recalling something very distant. "Jack Fawcett."

"What about him?" Christine asked. "Did you know him?"

He looked at her as if she were a backward child. "I was Jack Fawcett. Now I'm God."

"I'll be damned," Tony said, in wonder.

"Jack," Christine said excitedly, "I'm Brian's daughter. You're my uncle."

It was Jack's turn to look astonished. "Brian, my brother Brian . . ." he stumbled, trying to find the words.

"Yes," Christine said, "I'm your niece."

"My niece . . ." he breathed. "Where is Brian?" He turned around frantically, as though his brother might be hiding, waiting to surprise him. "I want to see him."

"I'm afraid he died several years ago," she said, as gently as she could.

"So long ago," he murmured. A tide of memory washed over him. In his mind's eye, he was again a young man, handsome, bold, with a fever for adventure and glory. All the manners and breeding of his upper-class background came back to him. Gallantly taking Christine's hand, he kissed it and said, "My dear, this is no place for a young lady. You should go home immediately."

"Do you think it's some sort of cultural universal that everyone disapproves of me?" Christine asked Tony.

"Stop whining, Chris. This is hardly the time or the place." Tony twisted Jack around. "If I let you go, will you give me your word not to run away?"

"I promise," Jack said solemnly. A fearful look came into his eyes. "But you can't be God, no matter what. I won't allow it." There was an hysterical edge to his voice.

"Fine," Tony said soothingly. "The job's yours. I don't want it." He and Raeder loosened their hold.

"Jack, what happened to Percy?" Christine asked.

"Eaten," Jack said succinctly. He tugged at her camera strap. "What's this?"

"A camera," she answered. "You take a picture and it's developed in a few minutes."

"Rot," Jack said. "I know about cameras. How old are you?" he demanded.

"Almost thirty." His rapid shifting from subject to subject left Christine rather confused. "You've been gone quite a long time, you know."

"Are you married?"

"No, I'm not," she said firmly. "Why?"

"Why not?" he countered. He looked at her suspiciously. "You're a suffragette, aren't you?"

"Something like," she said impatiently. "But we got the vote long ago. There've been many changes while you've been gone." She found it difficult to maintain a polite tone.

"Nothing like finding a long lost relative," Tony said in a suspiciously cheerful voice. "He'll get on famously with Lily, if we ever get out of this hole. A family is a wonderful thing."

"There's no reason for you to be enjoying yourself so much," Christine retorted. She thought of Jack, properly groomed and dressed, having tea with her mother. Her heart failed her for a moment.

"What, sir," Jack demanded, turning to Tony, "is your relationship to my niece?" Christine made an odd, choking noise.

Unruffled, Tony said, "She's my fiancée. We're to be married." Fortunately, Jack didn't see the look of astonishment on Christine's face.

"I see," Jack said gravely. "I don't approve of unmarried girls going off with men unchaperoned. I was young once myself." He nodded sagely. "No good can come of it." He wagged a reproving finger.

"Believe me, sir, I have the utmost respect for your niece. Nothing untoward has occurred and I hold her safety to be my most precious duty."

Christine gagged.

"We'll see," Jack answered gravely. Clearly, he was unsatisfied.

"This little reunion is all very touching," Raeder broke in. "And I'm sure Christine's virtue is a matter of great concern to us all, but there are some other issues I'd like to deal with, if you don't mind. For one thing, how did you get here?"

"The same way you did," Jack said. He stretched and yawned cavernously. Without another word, he went inside the hut, curled up in a ball, and fell asleep.

At daybreak, Christine and Manny gave up all pretense of sleep and joined Tony outside. Jack barely stirred.

"He smells like a zoo," Christine complained.

"What do you expect?" Manny asked. He looked at her disconsolate face and burst out laughing. "Tell me, Christine, is your whole family like him?"

"We tend to be better groomed," she retorted.

"I've never seen such a combination," Manny said. "Half the time he's a lunatic, and the rest of the time he's a very proper English gentleman. What a prude!"

"Let's remember that he's around ninety years old," Christine said. "He comes from a generation with a much different set of values than ours." She shook her head in admiration. "How he's managed to survive out here for so long, I can't imagine. He really must be a tough man. Who can blame him for being a little crazy?"

"Of course you are correct," Manny said. "I apologize."

"Do you think he can help us?" Raeder asked anxiously. "I am worried that he does not know how to leave here. Otherwise, why hasn't he done it?"

It was such a good question it immediately depressed all of them. "There's no point brooding about it," Tony said. "When he wakes, we'll press him for some information. In the meantime, why don't we do a bit of careful exploring? Perhaps we'll find something we can take back as proof of our find."

"Is it wise to leave him alone?" Manny said, jerking his head toward the hut.

"I think you should stay with him, Chris," Tony said. "He's more interested in you than the rest of us."

"I don't like being left behind, Tony. I should be with you."

"Please. Manny's right. Someone must stay

with him. If he wakes, you may be able to get some information from him."

Glumly, she agreed. With a sick heart, she watched the men shoulder their guns and disappear from sight.

"You know what I'd like to do?" Manny said. "I'd like to see where the *Triceratops* died. We could get a few bones to take back with us."

"How do you know we will ever get back?" Raeder said bitterly.

"Think positively, my friend," said Manny, clapping him on the back. "I think that old man knows more than he lets on. After all, he is God."

"He's nothing but a lunatic," Raeder muttered. He looked at Tony with determination. "I'm afraid I must add a hardship fee to my bill. You must pay me double what we agreed on. Never did I anticipate that my duties would include evading monsters. It was not specified when I agreed to come on this expedition."

"We didn't anticipate it either," Tony said. His mouth was twitching. "But I quite agree with you. You've more than earned the extra money."

Manny bit down on his lower lip, trying not to laugh. When he got control of himself, he added, "And you will share in our fame. Your picture will be in the paper, the women will call you a hero. Nothing, my friend, but nothing excites a woman so much as to be in the presence of a man whom the world proclaims as strong and bold. I have great experience in these matters.''

"Let's keep moving," Tony said. "We can't stand gabbing all day."

Their destination was close by. The huge carcass was lying in the sun, its bones exposed. When the wind blew toward them, the heavy, sweet smell of decay was overwhelming. Pterodactyls sat on the body, gouging out pieces of flesh. Small land reptiles gnawed at it.

Raeder moaned softly. "This is how we will end up."

"Shut up," Tony said. "You're still healthy." He looked at Manny. "Do you think we can get close? We'd have to beat off that crowd. Those birds, or whatever they are, are pretty aggressive. I'd rather not risk another encounter."

"I have just gotten a better idea," Manny said. "Look at the ground. You see those depressions? They are tracks. Let's trace them back a bit and see what we find."

"You are crazy!" Raeder said angrily. "We will find the brute that did this." He pointed toward the corpse.

"Perhaps," Manny said. "But we can stay out of sight. We are men, are we not? Should we not be more than a match for a dumb beast, no matter how large?"

"We can't capture a beast that size, no matter how small its IQ," Tony said.

"I understand, but I would like to see it again. It was fearsome. It will be a great challenge." He clapped his hand to his forehead. "We should have brought the camera."

He looked at Tony and his voice was eager.
"Let us stalk it. If it has a lair, then we will
come back again and take a picture. Think what
it would mean!"

Tony thought for a moment. "I suppose we
could track it for a bit. There wouldn't be any
harm in it." He looked at Raeder. "You needn't
come if you'd rather not. You could go back to
camp."

"I go nowhere alone in this nightmare
place," Raeder said emphatically. "I will go
with you. If you find something of value, then
I wish to be there to share in the claim. If I am
murdered, my blood will be on your hands."

"Terrific," Tony said. "I'll keep that in
mind." He paused for a moment. "It's a good
thing Christine isn't here. She'd never let us
do this."

"Your woman has more sense than you,"
Raeder said.

"That," Tony said with a sigh, "is very possible. Let's go."

Cautiously, they moved parallel to the tracks
that led into the trees. Crouching low to avoid
disturbing the feeding animals, they took careful measure of the footprints. The soft ground
was deeply sunken where the dinosaurs had
stepped, and there was a confusion of prints,
but it was easy to pick out the tracks of the
Tyrannosaurus.

"About two feet long, wouldn't you say?"
Manny said. His voice was unusually even and
toneless.

"I quite agree," Tony said, trying to sound
casual. "The claws must be seven, eight inches,

I should think. And look at the length of the stride—very impressive.''

Manny nodded. ''So, shall we continue?''

Tony cleared his throat. ''Absolutely.'' Raeder was muttering another prayer.

Continuing into the denser growth, they saw small streams with dogwood and evergreens growing along their banks. Berry bushes were all around and more of the palm trees. A small dinosaur that looked very much like an ostrich was feeding on the berries. It saw them and scuttled away, making odd hooting noises as it ran. There was a flurry of sound and a small group of ostrichlike dinosaurs exploded into view for a moment before disappearing again among the dogwoods.

''I'm glad there's something here that's afraid of us,'' Manny said. ''I was beginning to get an inferiority complex.''

The tracks led them along the water, downhill toward a small glen. There the footprints separated out, and the *Tyrannosaurus*'s led down farther into the valley.

''This seems to be where they joined up,'' Manny said. ''The *Triceratops* herd came from over there, crossed the stream, and went toward the plain. Then *Tyrannosaurus* must have gotten their scent while it was in the valley and gone after them. You can see how much shorter the strides are. They hadn't started running yet.''

''We use extreme caution from now on,'' Tony said. ''We have no idea what's back there. Let's try to avoid walking in the open. And keep a lookout for scat—not that it should be hard to miss from a creature that size.''

They moved back into the trees, walking as carefully as they could. Scanning the distance for any hint of movement, for any sign of the beast that was hidden somewhere in the forest, they crept forward.

Manny stopped in his tracks, holding back the others. "What's that?" he whispered. He pointed toward a tunnel-shaped mound of heaped-up mud and sticks. It was ten feet high.

"It looks like a kind of nest," Tony said. "Maybe one of those bird things lives here?"

"But why wouldn't they build their nests up high, like birds do?" Raeder objected. "This does not look as safe."

"Perhaps you're right," Tony said. He peered around nervously. "Do you hear something rustling?"

"Look at that," Raeder said, pointing toward the nest. "Something's coming out." For a moment, they saw only two feelers waving gently in the air. Then the rest of the body emerged.

It was an insect very like a cockroach, but close to a foot long. As it crawled quickly down the side of the mound, it made an odd, hissing sound. Others followed in quick succession. Their black bodies glittered. In a swarm, they headed toward the men.

"I think they're coming this way," Manny said, backing away. "Let's leave. We must have gotten into their territory."

They turned to run back the way they had come. The grass swarmed with more insects. They would have to wade through them. A few were climbing up their pants. Raeder gave a cry of disgust and brushed them off. A sudden, fierce pain ran up along his arm. He yelped. There was a neat puncture hole just above his wrist. An odd tremble, like a leaf fluttering in the wind, moved through his muscles.

"Get away from them," he yelled. "Their sting is poisonous." He stumbled, recovered his balance, and ran past Tony and Manny farther into the valley.

"Let's go," Tony said. They started running after Raeder. The rustling in the grass followed them. An insect dropped onto the back of Manny's neck from a tree limb. Cursing, he plucked it off. It bit him and he screamed. A few more climbed up his legs and settled on his bare chest.

"It's like fire,"he gasped. "We've got to find another way back. My muscles feel like they're going to cramp."

Raeder, still ahead of them, topped a rise, then disappeared abruptly down the other side. Looking down, they saw a slick of mud, with Raeder sitting at the bottom, his sides heaving in and out like a bellows. He was brushing off a few insects that were still clinging to his shirt and crushing them with his boots.

They followed him down. He looked at them and they saw his face was pasty and covered with sweat. "They do not follow here," he said. "I wonder why. Perhaps because there is something worse, that they are afraid of?"

"He's right," Manny said. "I don't hear them anymore. God, but those things sting like

the devil. The poison must be how they kill
their prey."

"Perhaps we should head back," Tony said.
"You aren't even wearing a shirt, Manny."

"I'm fine," Manny said. "If a few bites
were enough to scare me, I'd never get anywhere. Besides, there are more tracks. I want
to go on. I'm not afraid."

"What about you?" Tony asked Raeder.
"How do you feel?"

"I'll live," Raeder said. "I will not allow him
to shame me." He jerked a thumb at Manny.

"Shaming has nothing to do . . ."

"I want to go on," Raeder said abruptly.
"Am I any less of a man than you or that over-
sexed Don Juan?" His face was taut with anger, his eyes wild. "I have had enough of his
lectures and his superiority."

"Listen, you lousy, money grubbing, little
eunuch, I am tired of your whining." Manny's
voice was shaking with rage. "Here we are, lost
in this godforsaken place. Everyone tries to be
cheerful but you. Always you complain, always
you . . ."

"I tell the truth, which is more than you can
do," Raeder shouted. "You are too busy showing . . ."

"That's enough!" Tony said harshly. "I want
both of you to shut up. Save your animosity for
when we're back home, safe and sound. This
is no place for childish wrangling." He glared
at them. "Now, I don't expect you two to like
each other. For all I care you can spend every
private moment wishing each other in deepest
perdition, but I expect you to be able to rise

above personal differences and cooperate. Is that understood?''

Manny and Raeder hung their heads and mumbled. "All right then," Tony said. "If we're going, let's get on. I feel like a nursery teacher."

The tracks led them farther into swampy land. Their feet stuck in the mud and came up with a sucking sound that terrified them. What, they wondered, could hear them coming?

Ahead, there were heavy, labored, grunting sounds. They sounded like the engine of a truck stuck in a bog. For a moment they halted abruptly, as if someone had turned the key off. Then they began again.

"We're downwind," Manny said softly. "If we are quiet, it won't even know we're there. Come on." He pointed off into the trees, in a direction diagonal from the sound, where the cover was very thick.

Stooping low, they crept forward, halting every few paces. They barely breathed. When they were about a hundred feet from where they gauged the noise was coming, they parted the thicket of bushes and leaves and peered out.

The first thing they saw was a shallow depression about six feet wide. In it were some objects, white and oval-shaped. Squatting above it was the *Tyrannosaurus*. She was laying her eggs. Frozen in an inelegant posture, she was no less formidable than when they had seen her chasing down her prey.

Her mouth was open, clearly displaying the glittering, seven-inch teeth embedded in her huge skull. Her tiny eyes, sunk beneath ridges of bone, were cold and unreflective, seemingly indifferent to what was happening.

Her powerful legs, straining with the effort of birth, showed the massive muscles that had propelled her forward so swiftly. For a moment, the world swam before Tony's eyes. He was doused in a cold sweat.

"I've seen enough," he said. "We know where she'll be if we want her."

"Do they stay by the nest?" Manny asked. "Perhaps they are like turtles and forget about the eggs once they are laid. Or perhaps they are like crocodiles and stay to care for their young. It would be interesting to know."

"I really don't care," Tony said impatiently. "And I'm not hanging around to find out. My God, Manny, this is hardly the time for a natural history lesson."

"You are not a scientist," Manny said sadly. "Very well. I shall return later and get a picture."

"I want one of those eggs," Raeder said. "It would be worth a fortune."

"Now," Manny breathed, "that is a hell of an idea. It would set the scientific world on its ear."

"Are you going to go up there and ask her for one?" Tony demanded. "Excuse me, madame, but I'd like a dozen of your freshest, please? I'm leaving and so are you. We can talk about it later. We've still got to find another route back. Personally, I'd like to avoid our little six-legged friends back there."

"Look," Raeder said. "She's done. She's covering up the eggs."

The *Tyrannosaurus* stood erect and with her legs kicked a light layer of dirt over the nest. Her head swiveled on her massive neck, as if she were looking for anything that would threaten her brood.

Quietly, they retreated. They backtracked as far as the mud slick, then crossed the stream. They moved at an angle until they thought they'd avoided the insect nest, then headed back in toward camp.

By the time they'd returned, they were muddy and bedraggled. Christine was pacing back and forth in front of the hut. "Where have you been?" she demanded. "You've been gone for hours. I was frantic."

"We're all right," Tony said. "We just went for a hike."

"A hike? Where? What did you do?"

"Just wanted to get a better idea of the wild life," he said. "No reason to get in a lather. What have you been up to?"

She eyed him coldly. "You're hiding something. It's pathetic how transparent you are."

"Christine," Manny said, changing the subject, "can I borrow your Polaroid tomorrow? I'd like to take a few snaps."

"It's no good to you. I've used up all the film."

"You had almost a full roll," Manny protested. "What happened?"

"Uncle Jack got hold of it. You remember he wouldn't believe me when I said it developed a picture right away, so I showed him. He was quite fascinated. He's been fussing with it all day."

At the mention of his name, Jack came out from the hut. The camera was slung around his neck and he held a handful of photographs. Proudly, he showed them to the men.

Manny's shoulders sagged in discouragement. There were several photos of Jack that Christine had taken. The rest were ones he had taken himself. In Manny's estimation, they showed an unhealthy narcissism and preoccupation with self.

Aside from some rather skewed pictures of Christine and one of the hut, Jack had concentrated on photographs of his various body parts. It had been so long since he had seen himself, he'd decided he wanted a permanent remembrance of his various extremities. Manny stared at several pictures of feet, a rather lopsided shot of Jack's left hand, and closeups of toenails.

Undaunted by either modesty or technical difficulties, Jack had also taken several blurred images of his crotch. Finally, many of the photos were simply blank, or completely black.

However, looking at all the pictures as a whole, Manny realized that Jack was trying to do a complete inventory, so that he could put the pieces together like a jigsaw puzzle and have a larger representation of himself than the portrait Christine had taken.

Jack swaggered around, aiming the camera at random and clicking the shutter. Then, bored with the whole process, he returned into the hut.

Looking over Manny's shoulder, Christine pointed to the empty frames and said, "He was trying to take pictures of his face, but he couldn't do it. It's not easy trying to focus on your own nose.''

''How could you let him do this?'' Manny demanded. ''Now we have no film!''

''It's not so important, Manny.'' Christine looked at him hard for a moment. ''What did you see out there that it's suddenly so urgent you have the camera?''

Manny shifted uneasily from one foot to the other. ''A dinosaur,'' he said shortly. ''You know I wanted a picture of one.''

''Any dinosaur in particular?''

''We found where the *Tyrannosaurus* nests,'' he said, disgusted with himself for wavering. ''I want a picture and I don't see why I have to make excuses to you!''

She took a step back. ''You don't have to. If you want to get yourself eaten, it's your business. Why didn't you take the camera with you? We can't exactly run to the store and get another roll can we?''

''Will you two stop bickering,'' Tony snapped. ''What's gotten into everyone? Every time I turn around, you're at each other's throats.''

Manny and Christine stared at him. He wiped the back of his hand with his forehead. ''Sorry. I suppose I'm as jumpy as everyone else. Chris, were you able to get any sense out of Jack?''

''A little. He's been here so long, he believes he's created the place. It has something to do with him being the only person who's here. He says he thinks everything into existence. My guess is it's something like, 'If a tree falls in the

forest and no one hears it, is there any sound?'
The world only has meaning so long as Jack
invests it with some.

"He also told me that Raleigh died at the
Yanomani village, but that he and Percy *were*
the ones they brought to the temple. Percy, apparently, was very ill, and died not long after
they got here. Jack buried him, but one of the
local fauna dug him up and had him for dinner." She shuddered.

"Terrific," Tony sighed. "I'm sure this is a
fascinating story and Jack's mania will keep an-
alysts busy for years, but how did they get
here? Does he understand it? Does he know
how to get back?"

"That's what's so infuriating. He won't give
me a straight answer. I think he does know,
but he won't tell me. He gets this sly look in
his eye and starts babbling about how this place
is his creation and no one can take it from him.
I don't know what to make of it. Half the time
he's rational enough, but the rest of the time
he's incoherent. He keeps mentioning a letter."

"I'm going to talk to him," Tony said firmly.

"Good luck," Christine said.

"We've got to get the truth out of him," Raeder said. "What does he want? For us to be
marooned here with him for the rest of our
lives?"

"Let's see what we can find out," Tony said.
They crowded into the hut. Jack was placidly
eating a piece of meat and crooning over the
camera.

"Jack," Tony said in a stern voice. "We're

tired of playing games. How do we get out of this place?"

Jack peered at him through the tangle of hair, like an animal looking through a thicket, and a sly look came into his face. "The same way you got here."

"We don't know how we got here," Tony said, barely maintaining his composure. He looked at Jack thoughtfully for a moment. "Christine says you keep mentioning a letter. What letter are you talking about?"

"The letter to mother," Jack said. "Mother . . ." he repeated dreamily. "Ring around the rosy, pocketful of posy . . ." his voice trailed off and he stared blankly at his hands.

Tony tried again. "Jack, try to hear me. What do you want? Do you want to come back with us?"

Jack shook his head violently. "I won't abandon my creation. This is my world. Without me, it dies. You want to steal it," he said. His voice was low and menacing. "You'll corrupt it."

Tony got down on his knees in front of Jack. "We know you created this world and control it. We're asking you to let us go free. A god should be merciful. Don't you want your niece to go home, back to her mother? Don't you want her to get married?"

"She's a bluestocking," Jack said accusingly. "I never approved of intellectual females. Mother wasn't like that."

"God save us," Tony thought. "I'm going to strangle him with his own damn beard." He was suddenly struck with an idea.

"You sent the bone to Brian, didn't you? You

know how to leave this place and come back. Why won't you tell us?"

"I sent it before I was transformed," Jack said. "That was before I was God. I was only Jack. Then I came back. But I lost the gateway. It took me a long time to find it again. By then, I knew I was destined to stay here and take care of everything."

"If you tell us how to leave," Tony said, playing his final card, "we'll give you the camera."

Jack eyed him. "And will you give me all the turtle meat?"

"It's yours."

Jack pulled at his beard. After a long silence, he said, "I'll think about it. I was going to kill you, but maybe I'll let you go. After all, she is my niece. I will give you my decision tomorrow. Right now, I'm going to sleep." Without another word, he curled up on the floor and shut his eyes. He hugged the camera close to his chest.

"You son of a bitch," Tony said.

"Amen," Manny said.

10

Raeder woke before dawn. The others were still sleeping. No one had guarded the campsite the night before and he crept out of the hut unobserved. Everything was silent. He checked that his gun was loaded, then set off in the same direction he, Manny, and Tony had taken the day before.

Heavy mist covered the ground and the world was a dim, mysterious place. The white bones of the *Triceratops* shone dully in the half-light, making an eerie scenario. He paused by the carcass for a moment, surveying it, wondering if he should take a bone while he had the chance. Then, frowning fiercely as if he'd made up his mind about something important, he went on.

Traveling quickly, he skirted the area where the insects lived, slogging through shallow streams and marshy land. The trees and undergrowth dripped with water. Mud coated his pants and he was soaked to the skin. He listened intently for any noise that might betray a predator hidden in the thickets and fog, but he could hear nothing. Silence coated the world as thickly as the mist.

In the soft ground, Raeder spotted the tracks he and the others had made the day before. He looked down into the valley and swallowed hard. He balanced on the balls of his feet for a moment, as if he were being pulled forward and backward at the same time and could only maintain his balance by staying still.

Raeder was frightened. Every second he delayed made it more and more difficult for him to move. He was frozen to the spot. His limbs refused to obey his command to move. With an effort so strong it seemed he was breaking a set of invisible chains, he descended into the valley. As he walked, he muttered every prayer he could think of. And when he ran out of formal prayers, he repeated over and over the words, "Help me, please help me," appealing to any deity who would be inclined to show him some mercy.

Tony woke and stretched. He felt terrible. Every limb was stiff, his clothes stank, he stank, his cut arm itched, his teeth were furry, and he needed a shave. He also was starting to dream about food, just like Christine.

He had wakened just when he was about to be served a hot croissant with a pat of butter shaped like a rosette, a pot of coffee, and a bowl of fresh fruit cut into intricate shapes. The reality of cold, roasted turtle meat was not a decent substitute.

Manny was still sleeping, sprawled on his back, snoring through his open mouth. Christine was curled in a heap, and Jack looked like a pile of leaves ready to be burned. Tony scratched himself. He wanted a bath, clean clothes, and two weeks away from everyone, including himself.

Blearily, he looked around for Raeder. The hut was too small and boxlike to allow for hiding places. Trying not to step on anyone, Tony staggered outside, rubbing his eyes, but he couldn't see him. "Where the hell is he?" he muttered.

"Who?" Christine said, coming up behind him.

Tony jumped. "For crying out loud, Christine, would you mind not doing that? You almost gave me heart failure."

"Sorry. We certainly are in a good mood this morning. Who are you looking for?"

"Raeder." Tony shielded his eyes and scanned the distance. "I can't imagine where he's gotten off to."

"Maybe he's going to do what I am—take a bath. I don't care what's swimming in that damn pond. I'm going to get some of this filth off of me."

"It won't do you any good. Your clothes are a mess."

"I'll wash them. If I don't clean up, I'll go stark raving mad. Want to come along?"

"Might as well," Tony said with a sigh.

She took his hand. "It'll make you feel better."

Hand in hand they walked toward the pond. Carefully, they surveyed the water. Tony picked up a stone and threw it in to see what it stirred up, but nothing ominous rose to the surface.

"That's good enough for me," Christine said. "The way I feel, the Loch Ness monster wouldn't keep me out." She stripped and waded into the water, dragging her clothes after her. She shivered. It was very cold. Tony stood on the bank, watching her.

"You voyeur, you," she said, leering at him. "Come on in, the water's fine."

"Is that why you've turned such an attractive blue?" he asked. "It suits you. You've lost weight," he added, after a pause. "I can see every one of your ribs."

She shrugged. "I meant to diet, anyway. Besides, we're all thinner. Manny's down to the last notch in his belt and only modesty is keeping Raeder's pants where they belong. And you should see yourself, speaking of ribs." She grinned cheerfully. "This trip has done wonders for my waistline. I can't complain."

Tony took off his own clothes and entered the pond. He took a deep breath and immersed himself in the water. He came up blowing like a whale. Looking down at his body, he asked. "Does seeing me naked do anything for you?"

"You mean now, or in general?"

"Now, at this very moment. Do you feel like making love?"

She stuck out her lower lip, trying to evaluate her hormones. "Not in the slightest. Why, do you?"

"No. You'd think we'd be going at it like rabbits. After all, here we are in a totally unspoiled wilderness, with all sorts of pollen floating around, and no one to object, but it's the furthest thing from my mind. It's depressing.

"When I was in the Falklands, I used to think that what I missed most was women. I was fooling myself. I mean, here you are, and here I am, and what I'd really give my right arm for is a hot bath and a soft towel."

"We're not exactly in the Garden of Eden, Tony. There's no fruit hanging from the trees and the wildlife is hardly lying down at our feet and looking at us with adoring eyes. We're in a damn tight spot. Not to mention that we're half-starved and scared out of our wits. It must be male ego that makes you think you can get it up on a whim, divorced from anything as paltry as reality."

She splashed water over her breasts. "Besides, it's not really practical. It'd be a hell of a thing if I got pregnant in this place. I'm not keen on raising a child out here. The schools are lousy and I'm sure the poor thing's social development would be dreadfully stunted. How would it learn to play field hockey and make horrid ceramic ashtrays and all the other skills so necessary to a well-informed citizenry?"

Tony grinned a little ruefully. "I can see your point." He tugged at his beard. "Not to change the subject but do you think Jack will come across? What kind of game is he playing at?"

"I believe he will help us, Tony. I was thinking about it last night. He's just enjoying his feeling of omnipotence. But he'll get tired of it. Then he'll show us what a benevolent deity he is by letting us leave. After all, *noblesse oblige* is the hallmark of his class and generation. Scratch that dirt and underneath it you'll find the perfect turn-of-the-century British gentle-man.

"Also, it's been so long since he's seen peo-ple, he can't relate to them anymore except as part of his delusion that he runs everything here. And he can't stand competition."

"I hope you're right," Tony said.

"I think I am. He's getting rather sick of us, really. We're interfering with his megaloma-nia."

"I'll kiss his filthy knees if it'll persuade him to talk," Tony said with real fervor.

Christine laughed. "You pervert, you. I al-ways knew you were kinky." She glanced up at the sky. "That sun's burning off the fog. Let's lay these clothes out and give them a chance to dry a bit."

They sloshed through the water and back onto dry land. "I wonder where the hell Rae-der is," Tony said.

He hid in the thickets, too frightened to come out into the open. The piled-up dirt clearly marked the place where the eggs lay. Tensed, he tried to hear if the mother was nearby, but there was nothing. "Just go get it," he said to himself. "It'll be yours. You'll be famous. All you have to do is go out there and get one egg. How hard is that?"

Gently, he pushed aside the thicket of leaves and stepped toward the nest. He froze. A twig had cracked. He looked down. He was stand-ing on it. Forcing a laugh, he wiped the fine beads of sweat from his forehead.

The layer of dirt was so shallow he could see

the indentations made by the clutch of six eggs that was buried underneath. He reached down into the dirt and tried to lift one. He grunted. It was heavier than he thought. Slinging the gun over his shoulder by its strap, he slid both hands under the egg and lifted it from the nest, staggering a little from the weight.

The egg was hard like a bird's egg, rather than leathery like a snake's. It was almost three feet long, and seemed to weigh close to thirty pounds. The shell was ivory colored and rather rough. Cradling it close to his chest, he moved back into cover.

Raeder's heart was pounding with excitement. He was so elated, he felt lightheaded.

Retracing his steps, he began the trek back to camp. His progress was slow. Carrying the egg was awkward and he was terrified he'd drop it. The gun kept getting tangled in the bushes. His breath was labored and he began to sweat. Frightened that his hands would become too slick to carry it safely, he stopped periodically and gently laid the egg down to wipe them off.

As he neared the first stream he needed to cross, he stopped dead in his tracks. Something was up ahead. He could hear water being sucked up and stirred about and the heavy breathing of a large animal. He trembled and almost dropped the egg.

Cautiously, he put it down and crawled on his belly toward the stream. It was his worst fear come true. He was staring straight into the *Tyrannosaurus*'s open maw.

His heart skipped a beat. Apparently, the animal hadn't seen him. It was difficult to tell from those cold, unrevealing eyes what she actually saw. Her gaping mouth was scooping up water the way a steam shovel scoops up dirt. The tiny arms dangled in front of her, scraping the ground. Their puniness only emphasized the animal's immensity. The clawed hind feet flexed and unflexed, kneading the earth like a cat kneading a blanket.

Raeder crept back toward the egg. He embraced it, pulling it close. Panic swept over him. It was difficult to think clearly. He wondered if she would notice that an egg was missing, if his lingering scent and the hole left by the vacant egg would alert her to a predator near her nest.

The more he thought about it, the more frightened he became. He realized he was beginning to hyperventilate. Feeling ludicrous and hysterical at the same time, he pinched one nostril shut and tried to breath through the other. A friend of his in Buenos Aires had told him it was a way of handling stress. After a few seconds, he decided his friend was an idiot.

"Be calm," he said to himself soothingly. "Everything is fine. You are not going to be eaten by a dinosaur—it is absurd. This is the twentieth century." He stopped himself. "My God, what am I saying? This isn't any century at all. There aren't even any calendars."

Christine and Tony sat naked by the side of the pond, waiting for their clothes to dry. She tipped her head back and watched the clouds drift lazily across the sky. "There's a dragon," she said, pointing up into the sky.

"That's no dragon," he said scornfully.

"Certainly, it is. Look, there's the head at that end, and over there's the tail. The misty stuff at the front is smoke and fire coming from its nostrils."

Tony looked unconvinced. "I see a house over there. It's a country manor, as a matter of fact. There's a bay window, and there are the outbuildings. Over there is the kitchen garden, and there are the flower beds."

Christine looked at him incredulously. "Do you really see that?"

"Something like it. Perhaps I've embroidered it a little." He grinned. Then he looked at her. "Do you want to get married?"

She blushed. "Now?"

"Don't be obtuse. When we get back to London." He looked at her intently. "Lily would be delirious."

Christine looked down at the ground. "I don't know. I don't think that this is a good time to make a decision. I'd rather wait until life was a bit more normal."

"But it's taken these extraordinary circumstances to make me realize I should stop hedging and make a commitment. You're wonderful, Chris. I always knew it in my heart, but this trip has really brought it home to me."

"You're not so bad yourself," she said, kissing him on the nose. "But I'd really like to wait, Tony. Don't push me on this. I want you to want me as much in a London teashop as you do now, when everything is so terrible. It's much more likely the rest of our lives are going to be horribly mundane and boring. That's the sort of thing we've got to deal with. All this," she said, waving her hand about, "is an anomaly—I hope."

"Very well, madame," Tony said. "But remember, you had your chance. Once we get back to London, I may very well be swept off my feet by one of those Balkan vamps I was telling you about."

"Ve shall see about zat, my darlink," Christine intoned, lowering her voice a few octaves. "I haf my vays."

Tony snorted. "You're not even a countess. Can you offer me a house on the Riviera, mysterious assassins creeping through the shadows, exotic delicacies eaten on silken pillows?"

"How did the Riviera get into this? I thought she was Balkan."

"She's an exile, you dope. That's the reason for the assassins. It's clear you and I had different reading material during our formative years."

"E. Phillips Oppenheim was never my style. I always preferred E. Nesbitt myself."

"Hardly a preparation for one's more mature years," Tony said, putting his nose into the air. "Here I am ready to handle sexually sophisticated thoroughbreds while the best we can say for you is that you probably expect magical creatures to pop out of the sand and grant you wishes." He shook his head sadly. "No wonder you're such an escapist."

"How am I going to escape?" he thought. "I've got to get out of here." Then he heard the heavy tread of a large body moving over the ground. He lifted his head again and saw the upper half of the *Tyrannosaurus*. She was moving back into the valley, back to her nest.

"Shoo," he thought desperately. "Scat!"

Once she stopped and stared in Raeder's direction. Fortunately, she looked straight ahead, rather than down.

"Please God, don't let it look this way," he thought over and over. "Please, please, I'll do anything, I'll go to church, I'll give to the poor. Please let me live."

He hoped he was too small for the monster to notice. Everything else in this accursed place was more than twice his size even when he stood upright. Perhaps there was nothing this close to the ground worth her while.

The heavy footsteps receded and Raeder was alone. Quivering with fear, he picked up the egg, and crouching low, approached the stream. The dinosaur was already gone.

"Go," Raeder told himself fiercely. He splashed through the stream and sprinted awkwardly across an open patch of ground. His left foot caught in a piece of swampy ooze. The mud sucked at his boot, refusing to release it. He grunted and yanked it free. The egg wobbled in his arms.

He recovered and walked hastily toward cover. Mud that had leaked into his boot squeezed up between his toes and leaked out through the air holes.

When he reached a stand of evergreens, he breathed a sigh of relief. He felt like a fox being chased by the hounds. If there had been a hole to crawl in, he would have done it.

"Only one more stream and a few more miles," he told himself reassuringly. "Then you will be back at camp and you will be a hero. You will be able to condescend to Manny. You will find a way home and you will be rich. They will worship you as their hero. Your picture will be in the papers and there will be a song about you on the radio. All you need to do is carry the egg of an overgrown iguana back with you. Courage!"

From somewhere behind him he heard a terrible roar.

"I think these are dry enough," Christine said, patting the clothes. "By dry, of course, I mean more than damp but less than absolutely sopping."

Tony examined his pants. "I think the mud is a little less visible," he said dubiously. He shrugged and put on the wet clothes. "Do you remember dry, clean clothes?" he asked brightly.

"Only as a dim and distant memory," she answered, struggling with her wet trousers. "Give me a hand, would you? The damn thing is stuck around my bum."

Tony came over and yanked the pants up from the rear. "Thanks," she said, slipping on the wet shirt.

"Need any help buttoning up?" He reached toward the open shirt.

She slapped his hand. "I can manage, thank you. Come on, let's get back to camp. Hopefully, Raeder's turned up. Anyway, I want to start putting the pressure on dear old Uncle Jack.''

"Forward," Tony said. As they walked back, he turned to her and said, "Another reason you should marry me is that I'm probably the only man who knows all about your family and is still willing to propose. No offense, Chris, but I think many a man would rather face a breach-of-promise suit.''

"Tony, you're such a comfort."

When they got back to camp they saw Manny and Jack outside. Manny had rigged up a makeshift rotisserie and was heating up pieces of meat over the fire. Jack was once again looking at the photos he had taken, comparing each snapshot against its subject. Currently, he was intently studying, with a rapt expression on his face, his toes.

"Where's Raeder?" Manny said, looking up at them.

"We don't know," Tony answered. "He was gone when we woke up. We were down at the pond, trying to clean up a bit, but he wasn't there, either. I was rather hoping he'd have turned up by now."

"Wherever he went, he took a gun," Manny said, looking at him keenly. "He's up to something."

"Like what?" Christine asked.

Manny shrugged. "How should I know? I am not a mind reader. But a man like that, unsure of himself, bitter, anxious to recover his place in the world, is capable of many things. Jealousy can drive someone to surprising lengths."

"Do you think he's jealous of us?" Tony asked, uneasily.

"Of course. Witness that little scene yesterday. And he has been talking more and more about money, about using the expedition as a way to improve his finances. He does not say it jovially, as you and I would. He says it grimly. Also, he wishes to prove his manhood, I think."

"That's your fault, Manny. You're always bragging about your sexual prowess and your exploits."

"It wouldn't matter whether I did or not. He would still be jealous. I think perhaps his sex life is not good."

Christine rolled her eyes. "I really don't know what either of you are talking about."

"Forget it," Tony told her. "Manny and Raeder had a bit of a run in yesterday. It was nothing serious." He paused. "At least I think it was nothing serious."

"Do you think we should go after him?" Christine demanded. "If he's in trouble, we've got to help him."

"Let's give him a bit more time," Tony suggested, after thinking for a few moments. "If he does want to prove something, he'll only be even more angry and offended if we immediately assume he needs rescuing. He really does think Manny and I look down on him."

"I think I know where he went," Manny said. "He went after that egg."

"Oh, hell," Tony said.

* * *

Raeder plunged ahead, trying not to waste time looking over his shoulder to see if the beast was tracking him. He knew he couldn't outrun it, if it came to a chase.

The second stream was just ahead. He sprinted forward and jumped into the water. He hoped it would disguise his scent. He was wheezing, more from fear than exertion.

"Just a few more miles," he told himself. He refused to think about what would happen if he were hunted all the way back to camp. Just being among people would be a relief. Surely Tony and Manny could help him if the beast didn't give up.

"I am exaggerating," he thought. He forced himself to laugh. It sounded mechanical and false. "I do not know it is hunting me. I am frightening myself to no good purpose. Let us go on, calmly, with fortitude and presence of mind."

He peered out. Everything looked peaceful. Still trying to hug whatever cover he could find, he began the final march to camp. Unable to resist the temptation, he looked back. The *Tyrannosaurus* was snapping at the treetops, tearing them to shreds.

A whimper of fear escaped him. He turned and ran.

"Uncle Jack," Christine said in her gentlest, sweetest, tones, "could I talk to you?"

He looked up from his photographs, plainly irritated at being interrupted. "Go away," he said shortly. "You're always talking."

"Going away is exactly what we'd like to do. Only, you have to show us how. Remember, you said you'd tell us how we could get home?"

"Where's the other one?" Jack asked, suspiciously. "All of you have to go. I don't want you." He looked angrily at Tony. "He went to Cambridge, didn't he?"

Christine decided to ignore Jack's last remark and stick to the main point. "Mr. Raeder isn't here right now, but he'll be back shortly. Can't you tell us? We'll make sure that we take him with us. I don't think he'd want to stay behind."

"No, no," Jack said insistently. "All of you go together. I'll take you to the gateway and show you how to leave. That way I'll be sure you're all gone."

He gave her a disgusted look. "All of you are rather dull, you know. Father and I figured it out ourselves. That's how we sent the letter and the bone."

"You're much brighter than we are," Christine said through gritted teeth.

"I know," he retorted. He looked up at her again and his features softened. Staring intently at her face, he seemed to be searching for something he had lost long ago. His eyes seemed to focus.

"You're a nice girl," he said abruptly. He turned his head away, as if he were ashamed of himself. "It's not your fault. Everything is changed now. I know it."

Hesitantly, Christine laid a hand on his shoulder. He twitched, as if he would pull away, but he restrained himself. His mouth crumpled and a tear slid down his cheek.

Christine's heart broke. "Oh, Uncle Jack, please come home with us. It's where you belong. Don't stay behind in this terrible place. I'm begging you. We'll take care of you. You'll be famous."

He shook his head, slowly, sadly. "Too late, too late," he murmured. "My home is here now. Everything depends on me. I can't abandon my trust. You'll have to go."

He looked at her again, but his expression had changed. It was furtive and suspicious. The human spirit that had flashed into view for a brief moment was gone again, overshadowed by the madness that had gripped him long ago.

"You get the other one here and then I'll show you. No tricks," he said, nodding his head sagely. "No tricks. Pockets full of posey . . . one, two, three." He turned from her and went back to his photographs.

With a sigh, Christine went over to Tony and Manny. "He's going to show us how to leave," she began. Tony and Manny started forward eagerly. "But," she continued, "not until Raeder gets back. He wants to make sure he gets rid of all of us at once."

"Well, where is the scrawny bastard?" Manny demanded. "I say we go after him. Who knows how long before he changes his mind again?" Manny jerked his head in Jack's direction.

"Very well," Tony said, "I agree."

The camp was in sight. Raeder sobbed with relief. The last march had been a nightmare. Each time he'd thought he'd lost his pursuer, or it had given up, the gigantic head would rear up again over the trees. The grinning, toothy head, the dull, dead, fisheyes loomed above this world like the face of a god dedicated to implacable horror and senseless death.

He no longer believed he was being stalked by an animal. It was a demon unleashed from some ageless hell that hunted him for its own purposes; for reasons that had nothing to do with paltry human notions of sin and mortality.

"It's me," he shrieked. "I've come back, I've got it. Help me." He stumbled into camp, holding his precious treasure tightly to his breast.

Christine, Manny, and Tony rushed over to him. "Where the hell have you been?" Tony demanded angrily. "Who gave you permission to leave camp and take one of the guns?"

"Look, look," Raeder whispered. He gloated over the egg. "I have done this on my own."

Manny gave a low whistle. "I told you," he said, looking at Tony.

Jack came over to them. He saw what Raeder was carrying and his eyes widened. He looked anxiously in the direction Raeder had come from. "It's time for you to leave," he said decisively. "You've caused a lot of trouble."

"We're ready," Christine said.

Raeder looked at her questioningly. "He's going to show us the way home," she said, grinning. Raeder almost dropped the egg.

Jack cocked his head, as if he were listening to something. "Come," he said shoving them together like a dog herding sheep. "I'll take you to the gateway. Let's not dally."

They slid down the hillside, toward the place

where they had first arrived. Jack pushed them forward, not caring if they walked, stumbled, or slid, toward their destination. Finally, they stood on the knoll where they had hidden from the *Triceratops*.

A sudden bellowing rent the air. The *Tryannosaurus* was trampling the hut. She snapped viciously at the air, her head swiveling on her neck like a gun turret. Then she saw them and she charged. The ground shook as she ran, and clods of earth were torn up by the clawed feet. Her upper body was bent toward them and the tiny arms flapped with each jolt of her body.

"Get down there," Jack shouted, shoving them down the knoll. "Get into the depression."

They jumped into the bowl of earth at the base of the knoll. "What the hell do we do?" Tony shouted to Jack.

"Clap, you idiots, clap," he screamed back.

"Clap?" Manny said, bewildered. "What? Like this?" He smacked his open palms together.

In silence, the world shattered. The sun split in the sky, the earth erupted, their bones splintered and their teeth crazed into fragments. Stunned by the collision of the two worlds, they were once again overtaken by nausea. Then they collapsed on the temple floor. The crystal skulls grinned at them from their shadowy corners.

Coughing, wiping off their mouths, they managed to stand. Raeder still had the egg. It had made the journey undamaged. Frightened

that at any moment the room would disappear
and that they would again be hurled backward
in time, they moved hesitantly, afraid of disturbing whatever delicate equilibrium main-
tained the border between this time and the
other.

Tony was the first to recover his presence of
mind. Speaking softly he said, "I want us to
get the hell out of this room. Don't make any
sudden moves or loud noise. One at a time,
head for the door."

He nodded to Christine, who tiptoed to the
entrance and started down the steps. Raeder
followed her, then Manny, and Tony brought
up the rear.

At the base of the pyramid they saw their
camp, untouched, as if nothing had happened.
They stood in their own world, under the canopy of the Brazilian rain forest. By all outward
appearances, they had only been gone a few
minutes.

Christine slumped to the ground. "I'm in
shock," she said, shaking her head slowly back
and forth, as if to clear it. "Am I crazy? Did it
really happen? Did we dream it?"

"This is no dream," Raeder answered her,
holding out the dinosaur egg. Hesitantly, she
reached out a finger and touched it. "It's real,"
she murmured.

Tony rounded on him. "You almost got us
all killed because of that thing," he said heatedly. "Who the hell do you think you are?"

Raeder stiffened. "I have brought back the
only proof of our adventure. What else do we
have? Who will believe us?" He stroked the egg

gently. "This will make our fortune. Are you too foolish to see that?"

He looked at Tony defiantly. "It was I who braved the worst dangers, none of you. This egg is mine. I claim it for myself, to do with as I choose."

"It belongs to the expedition," Tony said flatly. "You know that. Don't try laying down new rules. Christine's money's paid for this trip, and your salary on top of it.

"And it's not a question of bravery. It's a question of discipline," he continued. "For all we know, that beast got Jack."

Christine gasped. "Oh no, do you think so?"

"Chris, I don't know," Tony said. "But he's an old hand at dodging the things, so if anyone could survive, it would be him. In all honesty, you couldn't get me to go back there at gunpoint."

Tony looked thoughtfully at the egg. "I'm not really sure who owns this. Is a *Tyrannosaurus* an endangered species if it's considered extinct, but it's not?" He groaned. "I can just see the lawsuits coming. We're going to have every government, every environmentalist, every scientist, on our backs until the day we die."

"It must be a very fragile point in the fabric of time," Manny said, talking to himself. "The skulls must maintain some sort of tension, and the sudden noise must disrupt it, tearing a hole in the continuum. Perhaps it is a question of resonance." He looked at them eagerly. "We can go back easily, any time we like. It is incredible."

"The implications are too dramatic to even

begin to contemplate right now," Tony said wearily. "I suggest we get some rest. Tomorrow, we're heading back. It's time to go home."

"Home," Christine breathed. "I never, ever thought I'd be so glad to hear those words."

11

The return trip was pure hell. The months of
river travel had left their mark. All of them were
exhausted and haggard. They stayed only a
single night with Jarivanu, who was delighted
and surprised to see them alive, healthy, and
no crazier than when they had left, but their
visit was marked by a sad event.

On their arrival at the Yanomani village, Jarivanu led them into a hut in a far corner of the
settlement. It was dark inside, and there was a
stench that seemed to soak into the air. A circle
of people stood around an old woman.

She was sitting on the ground, using a bundle of leafy twigs to fan her foot. As Christine's
eyes adjusted, she looked where everyone else
was looking—at the foot. Her stomach turned.

The top was an open pool of fluid with a
clearly defined shoreline of flesh. The woman
moved slightly as she fanned herself and yellow and black and red islets of infection slith-
ered to new positions on the watery surface of
the wound.

The sons and daughters looked at the newcomers inquiringly. A young man mimed
someone entering the river and treading on a

fish. She had stepped on a poisonous fish spine. Looking closer, Christine saw that her right leg was a dark reddish-brown right up to her thigh.

The old woman looked at them, her face resigned and dignified despite the pain, but her eyes were big and brown and pleading. It was a terrible moment.

Manny stooped to take a closer look at the leg. "It's gangrene," he said bluntly, trying to hide his emotions. He looked sick. "She needs massive doses of penicillin—far more than anything we have. Still," he looked at the intent faces of the people in the hut, "we have to give them something."

They rummaged through their medical kit and Manny gave the old woman two tubes of salve, a roll of bandages, and some vitamins. One of her sons pressed a plug of tobacco into his hand and patted him on the shoulder. Manny thought it was one of the worst moments of his life.

Outside, Manny spoke to Jarivanu. He turned back to the others. "She's dying—everyone here knows it."

"But can't we take her back with us?" Christine demanded. "Oughtn't we to get her to a hospital?"

Manny shook his head. "She wouldn't survive the trip and besides, she wouldn't want to go. She's never been away from her family in her entire life and the hospital is light years away, not just in terms of distance, but in terms of culture. If the journey didn't kill her, the shock would."

He was silent for a moment, and then said, "Perhaps time travel isn't such a rare thing as we might suppose. It's what we'd be demanding of her." He jerked his head at the hut.

"But what about flying doctors?" Tony said. "What about a helicopter?"

"For one thing, how are we going to alert one? Even if we had a radio, there's no one anywhere within transmission range. These people are so remote that for all practical purposes, they are living in the Stone Age. Don't you see that? Even if we could tell someone, no helicopter would land out here. It's much too difficult."

He stared off into the jungle, silent for a moment. "She's going to die soon and we can't stop it. Get used to the idea."

None of them could bear the idea of staying and watching helplessly while the woman died. They set off downriver the next morning. They were depressed. The problems, contradictions, and moral dilemmas of their lives pressed in on them more and more with each passing day. Also, the magnitude of their discovery terrified them.

The return trip is always worse than the original trip, Manny warned them. The bugs, the wet, the dangerous rapids, the poor food would still be there but now they were tired, with little enthusiasm left. All of them would have to be careful that frustration or simple exhaustion didn't kill them.

They were wise words, but difficult ones to follow. Each of them went through periods of sullenness and melancholy. Tension between Raeder and Manny grew daily. Raeder became more insistent that the egg was his to do with as he pleased. When they were only a week or so from a town, the argument reached a boiling point.

"I've had enough of this," Tony snapped. "We've been through it again and again, and I'm sick of it. When are you going to get it through your thick skull that everything is the property of the expedition? We don't have private claims. What I did, or you or Manny or Christine is not important. What matters is the organization—the Fawcett expedition, period."

Raeder's face was white with anger. "You are all so high and mighty. It is because you are rich. Do not try to deny it. You come over here with your money and your morals and your purism—it is because you can afford it. Hypocrites, all of you.

"You eat up the world and then, when someone wants a little piece of what you have, you lecture them on altruism and ethics." Unable to bear the tension of holding in his anger any more, he screamed, "Who the hell do you think you are?" He pounded his thighs with his fists.

All of them were shocked by this outburst. "Look," Tony said, trying to speak as calmly as he could, "let's all try to keep a rein on our tempers."

He looked at Raeder. "You will get everything we get. I swear to you we will split any money we get equally, and you'll be repre-

sented as a member of the expedition. We realize you went above and beyond the call of
duty on this trip.''

"You know what I think?'' Manny said. ''I
think they are going to laugh at us when we
get back. We have no real proof. If I hadn't
seen it with my own eyes, I wouldn't have believed it.'' He paused and scratched his beard.
''I *was* there and I'm not sure I believe it.''

"But we have the egg,'' Christine said.
''Thanks to Raeder,'' she added hastily.

"They will think it is another hoax,'' Manny
retorted. ''Just like with the bone you found in
the attic.''

"I do not think we will have the egg much
longer,'' Raeder said, rather reluctantly.

"Why not?'' Manny said. ''Is it going bad?''

"I don't think so.'' Raeder bit his lower lip.
''I think it is going to hatch.''

"You're joking, of course,'' Christine said,
swallowing hard.

"I hear noises inside,'' Raeder said. ''I sleep
with it in my arms . . .'' Manny snorted.

"Shut up,'' Tony said sharply. ''Go on, Raeder.''

"I can hear something stirring. The sounds
are feeble, but they are there, sometimes. Not
always. It is quiet for many hours, and then, I
hear it again.''

"Bloody hell,'' Tony said.

"What are we going to do if it hatches?''
Christine said. ''How big is a baby *Tyrannosaurus rex*?''

"From the size of the egg, I'd say about four

or five feet tall," Manny said thoughtfully. "We'll have to kill it."

"No!" Raeder said. "I won't have it. I found it. It's mine. It will be worth a fortune. If you kill it, I'll kill you." He glared furiously at Manny.

"That's enough!" Tony shouted. "I won't have these threats." He glared at Raeder. "I swear to God, if you don't learn to hold your tongue, I'll leave you here to find your own way back."

He took a deep breath, trying to get control of his temper. "We shouldn't kill it, if we can possibly help it. If Raeder is correct, and the egg hatches, this is the most important event in natural history since Darwin got on board the *Beagle*. We've got to do everything in our power to keep the specimen alive."

"What if it hatches while we're still on the river?" Manny demanded. "Where are we going to put it? There's barely enough space for the four of us, let alone a dangerous animal. It's a reptile, Tony. It comes complete with teeth."

"In *King Kong*, they tied a raft behind the boat and kept him on that," Christine said, rather timidly.

Everyone turned and stared at her. Then they stared at each other. "I will never again," Tony said, slowly and deliberately, "make fun of you for watching those movies. I'm man enough to admit when I'm wrong."

They made camp in the afternoon and built a raft, lashing the timbers together with vines.

Then they built as stout a cage as they could, tying it to the raft.

When they were done, they stood back to survey their handiwork. "Think it will work?" Manny said to Tony.

"I've no idea. If there were more rapids, we wouldn't stand a chance, but the river's pretty calm from here on in. I just hope that cage is strong enough. If the child is father to the man, we're in for a pretty formidable infant."

"Let's put the egg inside the cage," Manny suggested. "We shouldn't take any chances." Raeder looked at him suspiciously.

"You act like you laid the damn thing yourself," Manny told him. "You want to wake some morning with that thing in your arms? You'll wake up dead, is what will happen."

Muttering under his breath, Raeder placed the egg in the cage. He patted it solicitously. "It's moving," he whispered. They all bent close, staring at it through the bars. It seemed to wobble a bit, and there was a scratching noise coming from inside. Then there was silence again.

"We'll keep it in the cage," Tony said with finality.

A day before they arrived in the same small frontier town they had left almost four months ago, they were attacked. A large boat, holding ten men, shot out from a tributary where it had been hiding. Powered by oars, it moved swiftly and silently. It gave no warning anyone was lurking in the overgrown side channels.

Some of the pirates had long bamboo poles

with hooks on the ends. The rest had guns. While the armed men trained their weapons on Christine and the others, the ones with the grappling hooks pulled the expedition's boat toward them.

"Good afternoon," said one of the pirates. His English was passable. "We will have no trouble, yes?" He smiled at them brilliantly. "Otherwise, as the Americans say, you will make my day. I am very fond of American television. You will allow us to search your belongings."

A couple of his men dumped the contents of the packs and rummaged through them. They took the remaining cans of food, the guns and cartridges, and the money stowed at the bottom of one of the sacks and sealed carefully in plastic bags.

"You have very little. I am disappointed," the pirate said, counting the money. "It would seem you are returning from a very long trip, but you have brought back nothing." He leaned toward them, waving a rifle in tiny circles in Tony's face. "I wonder what would bring people like you to such a deserted part of the world? Is it gold? Drugs? Something else, something even more valuable?" Impossibly, his smile broadened. "Perhaps, if we have a friendly little chat, one of you will tell me? The lady, maybe, has something to say?"

"Hey, look at this," one of his men called. Using a grappling hook, he dragged the raft around so they could get a better look.

"It's a big egg," the pirate said, sounding bewildered. "What is the big deal about an egg?

Maybe it's a big bird, huh?'' He laughed, then looked around in disgust. "What's wrong with you guys? Haven't you ever seen *Sesame Street?*'' He spat in disgust.

The egg moved, rolling sharply along the floor of the raft. It shivered, as if seized by an inner convulsion. A crack zigzagged along the surface and then it shattered.

Uncurling from the split shell, the baby *Tyrannosaurus* took its first look at the twentieth century. And the twentieth century, in equal amazement, looked back.

It saw a scaly, reptilian creature five feet tall and weighing about sixty pounds. Its bulk seemed to be concentrated in its mouth, which was large, toothy, and open. The creature's opinions were expressed with a low hiss and a lunge. It hit the cage bars and fell back. It snapped its teeth.

"Looks like its mother, wouldn't you say?'' Christine said to Tony. "It has her mouth. And her temper.''

Shocked, the pirates shoved the raft away from them. The *Tyrannosaurus* staggered, then leaped again, rattling the cage bars.

"Let's get out of here," one of the pirates said to his chief. "I have seen many things, but I've never seen anything that looked like that. It is like a shark with legs.''

"Let's go, then," the chief said. He looked keenly at the expedition members. "It is very interesting what you have here.'' He nodded slowly, sagely. A smile curled his lips. "Perhaps we will see each other again.''

He nodded to his men and with a swift pull, the boat disappeared into the channel.

For a moment, they were too stunned to move. The dinosaur gave a low, gutteral cry, shocking them into action. "That was close," Tony said, swallowing hard. "They could have murdered us and no one would have been the wiser."

"Piracy is not uncommon on the rivers," Manny said. "Usually, they do not hurt you if you give no trouble." He looked at Raeder. "You know these parts better than us. Have you ever seen any of those men before?"

Raeder shook his head. "No. I do not think so. As you say, there are many thieves." He looked at the caged animal. "Perhaps it is hungry? Have we any food left?"

"Salted tapir meat," Christine said, pawing through the litter of their tumbled belongings. "And some smoked piranhas. Do you want to try to feed it?"

"Give me a piece of meat," Raeder said. Cautiously, he leaned toward the cage and dropped the meat onto the raft. Using a stick, he shoved it into the cage.

The *Tyrannosaurus* lowered its head and picked it up, swallowing the chunk whole. The jaws snapped, and drops of saliva splattered onto the raft.

"Let's give it the rest," Raeder said. "It seems to like it."

"Do you think we should wait and see if it agrees with him?" Christine asked. "He might be allergic to it, or something." She looked du-

biously at the creature. It was hard to think of
it having any sort of vulnerabilities.

"How do you know it's a 'him?' " Manny
asked her.

"Manny, I don't have a clue what it is," she
said. "I just feel odd calling it an 'it,' if you
know what I mean," she said, getting confused.

"If he starts gnawing on those cage bars, he'll
snap right through," Tony said, thoughtfully.
"Give it the rest of the meat. And we're going
to travel all night. We've a torch, and the last
stretch of river is pretty straightforward. I want
to get to a town as fast as possible. If we don't
stop, we should make land tomorrow morning."

So they traveled through the night, their precious find following in their wake, snapping,
snarling, and finally curling into a ball and
sleeping.

As Tony said, they came in sight of town in
the morning. After so long in the jungle, the
small town looked as busy and populous as a
big city. The streets and houses were a marvel.
The dim racket of a radio wafted through the
air.

A crowd of people were on the landing,
pointing and waving. As they got closer, they
saw that some of them were holding guns.
"What the hell?" Tony said.

"Oh God," Christine said. "Do you recognize any of those men? Take a good look at the
one closest to the end. The one," she said bitterly, "who's waving."

Manny leaned forward. "I'll be damned. It's our friend the pirate, complete with his merry band."

"Should we turn back?" Christine asked.

"Pointless," Tony said. "Where are we going to go? Besides, we're in firing range." He sighed. "Let's face the music."

The familiar grappling hooks reached out and pulled their boat into the shore. "Hello, hello," the pirate said cheerfully. "So glad you and your charge made it safely back." He reached out and helped Christine onto shore. "I am Juan Carias, Acting Deputy for the Under Secretary for the Protection of the Matto Grosso region, and I am impounding the entire property of your expedition." He pulled out an official card. "Welcome to civilization."

Juan's men brought them to a house at the far edge of town. He came in, all smiles, rubbing his hands, apologizing profusely for "any inconveniences this little official problem must cause." A couple of his men brought in pitchers of water and bowls of fruit. "Eat," Juan said. "Drink. Surely you are hungry?"

"Is this your other part-time job?" Tony asked him. "What you do when you're not busy on the river."

"They are all part of the same job," Juan answered smoothly. "Foreigners cannot simply run amuck through our country, taking what they wish, leaving nothing behind. I make a point to visit all the expeditions in this part of the world before they reach town. I would be remiss if I did not see if they were carrying anything illegal before they thought to hide it. There are many dishonest people about. It is shocking.'' He shook his head in a parody of remorse.

"Now, that creature you have with you is quite interesting. I have seen nothing like it. Surely you know there is a ban on taking rare animals from the country? You are not licensed hunters, you are not the officials of any zoological organization, you have no papers. I cannot allow it.''

He leaned toward them. "Where did you find it?'' He stared at each of them in turn. "I will have my answers.''

Tony looked him squarely in the face. "I wish to be put in touch with the British Consul.''

Juan laughed. "We all wish for many things in this life. We get few of them. Think about your situation. You are alone here, in a remote place. You have been on a long expedition to even less known places. If you never returned, do you think anyone would be very surprised?''

He sat back in his chair. "You would do well to consider your situation. Perhaps if I talk to each one of you alone, you will be more willing to cooperate.''

He looked at them like a man trying to decide on a piece of candy from a box. "You,'' he said, pointing to Raeder, "come with me.'' One of his men hauled Raeder up by the collar and took him from the house. "Excuse me,'' Juan said.

They marched Raeder at gunpoint to another hut. Juan came in after them. "Leave us,'' Juan told his men curtly. "See that we are not disturbed." He motioned Raeder to a chair at the table and then sat down himself. They stared at each other for a moment in silence.

Finally, Juan said, "So, Rudolf, what have you brought me this time?"

Raeder took a deep breath. "I have brought you the world."

Juan looked at him skeptically. "All you have brought is a bunch of people with nothing to their names but some beatup equipment and a . . . a . . ." He floundered, looking for the word, "A grotesque curiosity."

He sniffed. "The other expeditions had a great deal of equipment . . . cameras at least. Don't they even have a lousy camera? And then, of course, there were the prospectors, and drug smugglers."

Juan licked his lips. "These people are a complete waste of time. I am disappointed in you. All that babbling about riches and lost worlds, and how you had to go yourself. You are not a realist, Rudolf, that is your problem. You should have stayed here as usual, and let the Indians risk their lives."

Raeder shook his head vehemently. "You do not understand. I was right, right, right." At each repetition of the word, his first struck the table for emphasis. "What have you done with the animal?" he demanded. "It is critical you keep it safe."

"My men have put it in a cage that once held a jaguar," Juan said, with a shrug. "It is safe enough but I am afraid one of my men may lose his hand. The others only have bad scratches."

He waved his hands impatiently. "So, tell me, what is so special about it?"

Raeder lowered his voice to a whisper. "Have you ever heard of dinosaurs?"

"I don't like it," Tony said. "I don't like it one damn bit." He bit savagely into an apple.

Manny and Christine looked at him. "Do you think it's safe to eat that?" Christine asked. "What if it's drugged?"

"Don't be daft," he said.

"What do you think he's doing to Raeder right now?" Christine asked anxiously.

"Talking to him," Manny said calmly. He also took an apple and started to eat.

"You don't think he's being tortured, do you?" Christine said, utterly horrified.

"I doubt it," Manny answered in an ironic tone.

"Spit it out, Manny," Tony said. "What are you thinking?"

"I am thinking that our friend, Mr. Raeder, knows more than he says. I am thinking that Mr. Juan Carias is not such a stranger to him as he pretends."

"Why do you say that?" Christine demanded. "I know you don't like him but . . ."

Manny held up his hand to cut her off. "That has nothing to do with it. I have traveled often with men I do not like. That did not mean I distrusted them.

"It was last night," he said slowly, thinking back. "Something bothered me about his reactions to what happened. I couldn't put my finger on it, and it was just something in the back of my mind. I quickly forgot it, what with the arrival of our bouncing bundle of joy. But now, it comes to me."

"Well, don't nurse it, mate," Tony said sharply. "What's the problem?"

"He didn't complain," Manny said. "When has Raeder ever been faced by something frightening that he did not complain, and waver, and demand his rights? But last night, not a peep. It isn't natural, not for him, anyway.

"And another thing," Manny continued. "It was the same way when they took him out of here. Do you think he would go quietly? I don't. He would be begging and pleading and threatening and praying."

Manny nodded sagely. "He knows what's going on, mark my words." He paused as another thought struck him. "Do you remember how Carias said he 'visited' the other expeditions leaving these parts? Raeder would be an excellent contact for him, since he outfits some of them. Scientific expeditions often carry expensive equipment."

"Well, I'll be damned," Tony breathed. "Of course, we've no proof," he said hastily. "We can't convict him out of hand."

"Of course not," Manny said. "Although, at this point, I doubt if it matters what we think of him. He has the upper hand, not us. You'll see."

They waited—not sure what they were waiting for or what awaited them. They heard the guards shuffling outside, the low talk and laughter of the villagers walking by the house, a small plane overhead. They themselves were quiet.

Juan entered the house again, his smile as broad as ever. "So, my friends, have we come to any decisions?" He waited a moment. "No?" He shrugged. "It is no matter. Your Mr. Raeder was rather more cooperative. He had a most interesting tale to tell."

"Where is he?" Christine said angrily.

"He is safe and unharmed, I assure you. Do not fret."

"He's in it with you, isn't he?" Christine said angrily.

"Oh, Chris," Tony breathed.

Juan only smiled. "You have some intriguing ideas, Miss Fawcett. Do you suspect him of treachery? That is too bad."

"How do you know our names?" Tony demanded.

"Mr. Raeder has been a font of information." Juan beamed. He tapped his upper lip thoughtfully. "If what he says is true, you have truly come across a marvel. Such knowledge would make a man immensely rich and powerful."

His voice became dreamy. "Think of the untouched treasures, the oil, the gold, the minerals lying in the earth in their virgin states. Who could put a price on this hidden world?"

He looked at them. "I do not think such a secret should become common knowledge, do you? It might be misused."

Christine swallowed hard. "What are you going to do with us?"

"I haven't quite decided," Juan said. "Probably I will just shoot you and dump you in the river."

"Say cheese, everybody," a loud, raucous voice shouted. "Take a picture of those boys, Ted. Get the guns." A round, rather red face, poked into the hut. "Peekaboo, I see you," it shouted, laughing and wheezing at its own voice. A body appeared, raised a camera, and took a snap. They were momentarily blinded by the flash.

"Mr. Farragut," Christine gasped, when she could see. Tony and Manny gaped.

"Who the hell are you?" Carias demanded.

"Thomas Farragut, reporter, *London Sun*," Farragut said, grasping Juan's hand and moving it up and down like a pump handle.

"You are the press?" Carias said, aghast.

Farragut winked. "You got it, mate." He pointed at Christine. "This little lady has been great copy, on and off, for months." He nodded emphatically. "My paper, which, I might add, has one of the largest circulations in all England, has sent me down here to welcome the returning heroine and her stalwart, handsome lover back to civilization. She's been through quite a lot, you know."

"You don't know the half of it," Christine murmured.

"Neither do you," Farragut said enthusiastically. "The headlines have been terrific. We've followed your entire trip—in our imagination, of course. 'Lady Explorer Fearlessly Follows in Family Footsteps'—that was for starters. It refreshed the public's memory about your grandfather and his nutty theories. It was wonderful—Atlantis is very popular right now.

"Then we followed that with 'Amour in the Amazon—A Woman's Tale of Lust and Love'. That was about you and Mr. Blondell, here. We made sure to get his service record in and how he's a war hero. Very romantic." Tony groaned.

"After that, we had 'Bigfoot Wants My Body,' with a very nice picture of Ms. Fawcett, I must say." Christine's mouth dropped. "Well," Farragut said, "your face, anyway. We tacked it onto some other girl's body—someone with a few more thems and thoses, if you get my meaning." He winked.

"Bigfoot is in the United States," Manny objected. It was the only sane thing that came into his mind.

"Oh, now, we can't be sure, can we? You got his address? 'Course not. Maybe it was his cousin. Why, I bet you saw all sorts of things out there you couldn't identify. Isn't that right?" He looked appealingly at Christine.

"You bet," she said.

"There, you see," Farragut said triumphantly. "And how do you know what they did or didn't want?"

A large, rather gangling young man ducked into the hut. He grinned, a little sheepishly. "Hullo," he said.

"Hello, Ted," Christine said, rather faintly.

"My nephew, Ted," Farragut said. "Sister's boy, you know." He winked again. "And who are you, sir?" he asked Carias. "Want to get your name in the paper, don't you? None of

that boring, official, 'no comment' stuff, right?
Ted, get a picture of the gentleman." There was
another burst of light. Ted grinned happily.

"Loves to do that, he does," Farragut said
proudly, clapping his nephew on the back.

"Excuse me," Carias mumbled. "This is not
official. I must make inquiries. I was not noti-
fied." He dashed out of the hut.

"Well," Farragut said, looking after him,
"what's his trouble?"

Christine flung her arms around Farragut and
kissed him.

For perhaps the first time in his life, Tommy
Farragut was speechless.

"Mr. Farragut," Christine said, laughing, "I
don't know if I should thank you or give you
the name of my solicitor and threaten you with
a libel suit."

"Many of our subjects feel like that," he said
contentedly. "No one wants to admit to liking
publicity. Say, is that your little pet out there?
The thing jumping up and down in the cage,
with all the teeth? It'll make a great picture.
Has it made any improper advances toward
anything?" he asked hopefully.

"By the way," he rattled on, "if you folks
want a lift to Cuiaba, I'm your man—price of
admission is an exclusive interview with the
brave explorers. Got my own private plane out
there. Say, but isn't this the most godforsaken
country you've ever seen? Christine, you hav-
en't been molested or anything have you?"

Tony, Christine, and Manny sat comfortably
in their first-class seats on the British Airways

flight to Heathrow. Christine was sipping a cocktail. Manny and Tony were drinking beers.

"Where do you think Raeder and Carias vanished to?" she asked. "Not that I really care much." She stretched luxuriously in her seat.

"It's not hard to disappear in the rain forest," Manny said. "They both know their way around. I doubt if they will ever be found—unless they want to be."

"Do you think they'll go back to the temple?" Tony said, frowning. "It's really too bad they got away. Think what kind of havoc they could cause."

Manny shrugged. "What can we do? We are in for a hot time ourselves. The Brazilian government has many questions they want to ask. So does the British government, and so does everybody else."

The plane bounced a bit. "That was an air pocket, right?" Christine said.

"What did you think it was?" Tony asked.

"I thought it might be Rex, bouncing around in the baggage compartment. I can't believe they agreed to ship him back to England."

"Rex?" Manny asked.

She shrugged. "We have to call him something. And it's short for *Tyrannosaurus rex*, after all. What do you think we should call him? Muffin?"

She took another sip of her drink. "I hope he'll be all right in quarantine. How long do you think they'll keep him under observation?"

"Months," Manny said emphatically. "Introducing a new species into an environment is extremely dangerous."

"Well, they're not going to turn him loose to roam about Hampstead Heath," Tony said.

"It doesn't matter," Manny said. "They bring with them diseases, parasites, infections, against which our animals have no defenses. And it works both ways."

"You don't think he'll be in any danger, do you?" Christine said anxiously. "I feel rather guilty about him. If I had it to do over, I would have left him in his home, where he belongs."

"We shall see what we shall see," Manny said, cryptically.

"Do I look any different?" Christine asked, turning to them both.

"Thinner," Tony said.

"Tired," Manny answered.

Christine sighed. "Shouldn't I be marked by an air of mystery and hidden knowledge? Shouldn't all of us? Think of all we've been through, of what we've seen."

"Now you do sound like you've been reading Oppenheim," Tony said.

"I think the changes are in the heart," Manny said. "And in the mind. Inside, we are different and so, for us, the world is different, even if we do not look different to the world. We cannot see the things the way we did before." He looked a little sad. Then, shaking off his mood, he smiled.

"But, why should I be melancholy? We are still alive, and our friendship has grown and strengthened." He raised his beer. "To those things which time has strengthened instead of destroyed. To love, to passion, to friendship."

They raised their drinks in a toast.

WORLDS OF WONDER

☐ **THE HISTORICAL ILLUMINATUS CHRONICLES, Vol. I: THE EARTH WILL SHAKE by Robert Anton Wilson.** The Illuminati were members of an international conspiracy—and their secret war against the dark would transform the future of the world! "The ultimate conspiracy ... the biggest sci-fi cult novel to come along since *Dune.*"—The Village Voice
(450868—$4.95)

☐ **THE HISTORICAL ILLUMINATUS CHRONICLES, Vol. 2: THE WIDOW'S SON by Robert Anton Wilson.** In 1772, Sigismundo Celline, a young exiled Neapolitan aristocrat, is caught up in the intrigues of England's and France's most dangerous forces, and he is about to find out that his own survival and the future of the world revolve around one question: What is the true identity of the widow's son? (450779—$4.99)

☐ **THE HISTORICAL ILLUMINATUS CHRONICLES, Vol. 3: NATURE'S GOD by Robert Anton Wilson.** These are the events which will soon reshape the world ... (450590—$4.99)

Prices slightly higher in Canada.

If you and/or a friend would like to receive the *ROC Advance*, a bimonthly newsletter featuring all the newest and hottest ROC books and authors, on a complimentary basis, please fill out this form and return it to:

ROC Books/Penguin USA
375 Hudson Street
New York, NY 10014

Your Address
Name _____
Street _____ Apt. # _____
City _____ State _____ Zip _____

Friend's Address
Name _____
Street _____ Apt. # _____
City _____ State _____ Zip _____